"Behave yourself, you jerk," she whispered.

When post time finally arrived, Leslie saw from the odds board that the bettors didn't have any confidence in Battlecry either—he was going off at 80 to 1! The odds would have been even higher, but one three-year-old in the field had never raced at all. Battlecry at least had been on a racetrack. But the big horse hadn't impressed anyone with his behavior in the walking ring. Physically, he was beautiful—tall, elegant, with his coal black coat shimmering and his long mane and tail flowing like silk. But it had been all Leslie could do to control him as he skittered around and jerked at the lead shank. He'd worked up a nervous sweat before his petite, dark-haired jockey even mounted. She hadn't looked too happy as she'd settled in the saddle, but she hadn't let Battlecry get the better of her. After listening carefully to Mr. D'Andrea's instructions, she nodded, then said quietly but firmly to the horse, "We're going out there and you're going to run a good race!"

But as Leslie looked down from their grandstand seats and watched the field go into the starting gate, she felt a lump rise in her throat. Suddenly, the gate d̶ ̶ ̶ ̶ ̶ ̶ ̶ ̶ ̶ ̶ ̶ ̶ ̶ ̶ ̶ringing bells. The race was o

D1112966

Collect all the books in the **Thoroughbred** series, by bestselling author Joanna Campbell

BATTLECRY FOREVER!

JOANNA CAMPBELL

HarperPaperbacks

A Division of HarperCollins*Publishers*

HarperPaperbacks *A Division of* HarperCollins*Publishers*
10 East 53rd Street, New York, N.Y. 10022

Produced by Daniel Weiss Associates, Inc.
33 West 17th Street, New York, New York 10011.

First Printing: March 1992

Printed in the United States of America

HarperPaperbacks and colophon are trademarks of
HarperCollins*Publishers*

10 9 8 7 6 5 4 3 2 1

1

Leslie D'Andrea stared, entranced, at the powerful black Thoroughbred on the other side of the crowded auction pavilion. Impatiently she pushed a strand of long blond hair out of her eyes as she watched him prance arrogantly around his holding paddock. He was beautiful—tall and muscular, yet graceful. When he flung up his finely shaped head, his mane flew out like a cloud of silk. His black coat was barely visible beneath the layer of dust kicked up by the multitude of hooves. He stood out from the other horses like a polished diamond dropped on rough pebbles. Leslie felt totally and utterly drawn to him.

But what was he doing here? He didn't belong at this New Jersey auction, where most of the Thoroughbreds were worn, tired failures from the racetrack. After all, many of the buyers were from slaughterhouses, buying horses by the pound!

Leslie prodded her father, who was standing beside her. "Look at him! What do you think?"

Her father glanced up from his auction program. His dark eyes followed her pointing hand. "You mean that black?" he asked.

"Yeah. He looks much too good to be here."

Her father scowled. "Mmm, he does. Let's check him out." Phil D'Andrea was a respected New York trainer, as his father had been before him; at fifteen, Leslie was following in their footsteps. The D'Andreas also ran a rescue operation on their farm, supported almost solely by private contributions. The horses they bought today would go to the farm to be retrained as pleasure horses, then sold to good homes.

Leslie and Mr. D'Andrea pushed their way through the crowd of buyers, who were dressed against the chill of the February evening. In the holding paddocks horses stomped, snorted, and cried out shrilly. Dust hung in the air, which was heavily scented by horse—and fear. Leslie hated the auction's atmosphere, and she was feeling the stress now, even though she and her father were there to save some of the unwanted animals.

The big black horse was standing by the paddock rail. He laid back his ears in warning as they approached.

"Easy there," Leslie murmured. "We just want to take a look at you. You're gorgeous, aren't you?" Now that she was near the horse, she was even more impressed. He stood close to seventeen

2

hands high, solid and strong. His eyes sparkled with intelligence. "You're something else," Leslie said. "And I think you know it."

The horse eyed her warily, but his ears pricked forward as he listened to her voice. Leslie could already picture him on their farm—with her in his saddle. She had ridden from the time she could walk and was expert enough to assist her father by riding his string of horses for their workouts.

Her father ran his fingers through his thick tawny hair and grunted. "Well, he's got decent conformation and he looks healthy enough—but geez, he's a stallion! What's he doing in with a bunch of third-rate overraced geldings?" He flipped through his auction program. The horses were listed by hip numbers corresponding to the numbered tag pasted to their rumps. He found the black horse in the program, and Leslie eagerly leaned over to read the brief description. "BATTLECRY, black horse, 5 years old, sire War Drum, dam Summer Song."

"The name fits him," Leslie said.

"We don't buy horses on the basis of their names."

"I know, but he looks fantastic too."

"What would we do with a stallion?" her father said thoughtfully. "They're high-strung and unpredictable. None of our buyers would be interested, and he'd be pretty hard to handle."

"Can't we at least find out more about him?" Leslie asked.

"I don't know, Leslie. I've already picked out five or six horses to bid on—all of them fit and retrainable. I really think this guy would be too much of a handful."

Leslie couldn't believe her father's reaction. "But he's the best horse here!" The thought of the big horse possibly going to the butcher made her feel physically ill. She made an instant decision. "I could take care of him myself. He'd be *my* responsibility. I'd have the time in the afternoons to retrain him."

Her father saw the determined expression on her face. "Hmm. Well, let me see what I can find out about his background. But remember, we can't afford to save every horse here—as much as we'd both like to. I'm making no promises."

Leslie's stomach was knotted in a ball as her father moved off. Battlecry had ceased his restless pacing and was watching her—almost as if he understood that she was trying to save his life. His ears were pricked in her direction, and his delicate nostrils flared as he tried to catch her particular scent. Then he snorted and vigorously bobbed his sculpted head.

"Yes," she whispered. "I can see you're special. I'll do what I can for you." The horse bobbed his head again, then paced out a tight circle in the paddock. His body vibrated with barely contained energy. But there was fear in his eyes, too. He sensed the danger ahead.

Suddenly Battlecry let out a loud and challeng-

4

ing whinny. Several of the horses near him moved nervously away. Then the big horse stopped in his tracks, with feet firmly planted, and stared at Leslie.

"I know. You need help. Somehow I'll convince my father to buy you." She just prayed she could.

Leslie jumped when her father tapped her shoulder. "They're ready to start the sale. Let's go find some seats."

"What did you find out about him?" Leslie asked breathlessly. She could barely take her eyes off the stallion. He was a chance in a million! She cast a long look back as she followed her father. The horse was still watching her, an unfathomable expression on his face.

"He's consigned with a string from Frank Hawkins's barn," Mr. D'Andrea said.

Leslie knew who Frank Hawkins was. He was a trainer based at the New York tracks—gray haired, potbellied, and loud. She'd never thought much of the way he handled his horses. He didn't seem to have any real feeling for them.

"The owners went bankrupt, and they're selling off all their stock," her father continued. "The horse is sound enough, and he's raced, but he's got a miserable reputation. He's moody and unmanageable. He acts up in the gate and has been known to throw riders for the pure fun of it. When he actually gets on the track, he won't settle and has finished dead last in every race he's been in. Hawkins wanted to geld him to quiet him down, but the owners refused. Guess they were hoping they could breed him, though his bloodlines aren't anything special."

With each of her father's words, Leslie felt the knot in her stomach grow.

"When the owners went bankrupt," her father added, "Hawkins decided to wash his hands of him."

"He's still too good a horse to be sent to the butcher!" Leslie cried. "He's probably been handled badly. You've said you don't respect Hawkins as a trainer. Let me try to turn him around. I know I can!" She *didn't* know that for sure, but suddenly she desperately wanted to try.

"He's not the kind of horse who's going to be easy to retrain," her father said. "From the sound of it, he's been getting away with murder for a long time. He'll be set in his ways. Even if he were gelded, he'd be a risk."

"Please, Dad. We can't let him go to the slaughterhouse!"

"That won't necessarily happen. Another private bidder may be interested in him."

Leslie gave her father a pleading look.

"Oh, okay. I'll think about it," he conceded finally. "I'll see how the bidding goes on the other horses I've picked out."

Leslie had to be content with that as they took their seats. But she was all nerves as the first hip number was called and the bidding began.

She watched with a heavy heart as the horses

were brought forward into the ring, one after another. They looked terrified—snorting and skittering, with the whites of their eyes showing. Through some animal instinct they knew that their fate was probably not good. Most horses sold for only three or four hundred dollars; some for less. The bidding went quickly, with the auctioneer's singsong interrupted only by the pound of his gavel as the sold horse was led off and another brought forward. There were several private buyers in the audience. Mr. D'Andrea was top bidder on two mares and three geldings, all nice-looking animals. But Leslie was sickened to see that many of the horses were going to the slaughterhouse. She knew those buyers from previous visits to the auction, and her eyes stung as she watched the ill-fated horses being taken away. They'd be loaded in tight quarters on a livestock truck like so many head of cattle.

Her hands grew clammy as she waited for Battlecry's hip number to be called. Her father had already bought five horses. She glanced up at his face, but he was staring at the podium, concentrating on the bidding.

Then Leslie felt her throat close as she saw Battlecry being led forward. He didn't go willingly—he balked and fought the handler, swerving his back end from right to left. When he reached the ring, he reared suddenly and slashed the air with his hooves, pulling the lead shank through the handler's fingers. A second handler rushed forward to grab the other side of the stallion's halter when his feet touched the ground. Leslie winced as the two handlers loudly cursed the horse.

Their words seemed to infuriate him. He lunged against their hold with a screeching cry. To Leslie he looked magnificent—even majestic. And his antics woke up the audience. A murmur rippled through the crowd.

The auctioneer wasted no time. "All right, what am I bid . . ." he sang out. "Start it at two . . . I have two . . . two and a half . . ." A program was flicked. "Now two and a half . . . can I have three . . . let's go three . . . three now . . . I have three . . . three fifty . . . I have three fifty . . . three seventy-five . . ."

The auctioneer was talking so quickly, Leslie could barely keep track of the bidders. But she knew one of them was from a slaughterhouse, and her stomach tightened.

"I have three seventy-five," the auctioneer called. "Do I hear four . . . let's make it four . . . a lot of horse for three seventy-five . . . no interest at four?"

Leslie couldn't believe it. Why were they letting the stallion go so cheap? And the slaughterhouse representative had the highest bid!

"Three seventy-five once . . ."

"Dad!" Leslie gasped hoarsely. Suddenly her father's hand shot up. "Four."

"I have four . . . do I hear four and a quarter?"

8

The meat packer nodded.

"I do . . . and now four fifty . . . four fifty anyone . . . can I hear four fifty? Four twenty-five once . . . four twenty-five twice . . ."

Leslie grabbed her father's arm. He couldn't let this happen! Battlecry would go to the slaughterhouse if he didn't bid higher.

Her father lifted his program. "Four fifty."

Leslie almost fainted with relief, but she held her breath as she looked at the other bidder. For a long, agonizing moment he seemed undecided, then he shook his head. Leslie started to breathe again.

"Four fifty once . . . four fifty twice . . . *sold* to the gentleman in the third row." Mr. D'Andrea held up his bidding number. "Number thirty-six," the auctioneer called to the clerk who was recording all the sales. "Next!"

"Thanks, Dad! Thanks so much!" Leslie cried. She was trembling all over.

Her father made a wry face. "Well, that cleans us out. Buying him put me over what I wanted to spend. Let's pay up and get our horses. And remember, he's your responsibility. If he turns out to be as big a terror as I think, I'm finding another home for him."

Leslie rose and hastily followed her father. She wasn't about to say another word. She had what she wanted. She had the big black fireball. Now she only prayed that she really *could* turn him around.

Her father's lanky young training groom, Jeremy, met them at the exit door. He shook his red head and leaned over to whisper in Leslie's ear, "Buying that last one was your doing, wasn't it? You gotta be crazy!"

"Wait and see what I do with him!" Leslie whispered back.

"Hmph."

"We're number thirty-six," Mr. D'Andrea told Jeremy.

"Right," Jeremy said quickly. "I'll start loading them." He hurried in the direction of the paddocks containing the sold horses. Each was marked with the buyer's bidding number.

"You'd better let Leslie help you with that black!" Mr. D'Andrea called after him. "You'll need it."

They spent the next half hour loading and settling their new acquisitions in their six-horse van. By unstated agreement they decided to load Battlecry last, to put him in the sturdiest of the stalls at the front. Leslie approached the still excited stallion first, talking to him and trying to calm him down. His experience on the auction block had turned him into a bundle of nerves.

"You remember me," she told him softly. "There's nothing to be afraid of now. You're coming to a good home."

The horse snorted. The whites of his eyes showed as he watched her and pawed the ground with a front hoof. But he seemed to recognize her.

10

"Easy, boy . . . look what I've got." Leslie reached in her jacket pocket and pulled out a sugar cube. When they were vanning horses, she was always prepared with treats. Many balked at being loaded and needed to be bribed.

Battlecry widened his nostrils and sniffed. He knew exactly what Leslie had in her hand. Forgetting himself for an instant, he stretched out his sleek neck and delicately lipped up the cube. Leslie instantly grabbed his halter and clipped on the lead shank. He reacted just as quickly by throwing up his head and squealing in outrage. But Leslie had the shank clenched firmly in her gloved hand and managed to hold the backing horse while Jeremy clipped a second shank to the other side of his halter.

The stallion was really infuriated now. With a whipping motion of his neck, he flung his head around and fastened his teeth into Jeremy's shoulder.

"Yow!" Jeremy cried. The horse immediately released him, but Jeremy had lost his grip on the shank. Mr. D'Andrea rushed over and grabbed it.

"I've got him. You all right?"

"He would have drawn blood if I wasn't wearing a jacket!" Jeremy stormed. "Idiot."

It took every ounce of their strength and patience to get the stallion as far as the side of the van. "Get those leg wraps on him while we hold him," Mr. D'Andrea told Jeremy.

"Me?" Jeremy protested.

11

Mr. D'Andrea glared at him, and Jeremy hurried to pick up the protective wraps lying beside the van. Leslie had to bite her lips to keep from giggling at Jeremy's expression as he approached the horse. She'd never seen Jeremy work so fast as he knelt beside each leg, fastened the Velcro strips on the bandage, and jumped away before he got kicked. It took another fifteen minutes to get the stallion loaded and in crossties in the stall. He was still snorting out angry protests as they secured the van door. They all breathed a sigh of relief as they climbed into the front seat of the van, and Mr. D'Andrea started the engine. But as they hit the highway for the hour's drive back to Long Island, they repeatedly heard the crash of iron-shod hooves.

"If that guy wrecks my van or excites the other horses, I'll personally strangle him," Mr. D'Andrea growled.

Leslie cringed and glanced over at her father in the driver's seat. She knew he didn't really mean it —not yet, anyway. But his next words didn't encourage her.

"I hope I haven't made a *big* mistake."

2

Leslie was just finishing her breakfast Sunday morning when she heard her father shout from the stable yard, "Leslie, get out here!"

She jumped up, grabbed her jacket from its hook in the back hall, and rushed through the door. The tone of her father's voice could only mean more trouble with Battlecry. He'd been on the farm only one full day, and he was already living up to his reputation.

Mr. D'Andrea was standing on the other side of the drive, near the barn and paddocks that housed their rescued horses. He was holding Battlecry, and he didn't look happy.

Neither did Battlecry. The stallion danced at the end of the lead shank and thrust up his head, trying to break her father's strong grip.

"What's wrong?" Leslie cried as she ran up beside them.

Her father gave the horse a grim look. "He got out of the paddock last night. Edwin found him in with the mares."

"Oh no." The weather had turned unseasonably warm the day before, and they'd put Battlecry out in one of the small paddocks for the night. Several mares had been left in a nearby pasture.

"Oh yes," Mr. D'Andrea growled. "That, on top of him biting Jeremy, nearly kicking out my van, and almost throwing you yesterday. This guy's a real piece of work!"

"But how did he get out?" Leslie exclaimed. She knew their stable manager, Edwin Monroe, would never have left the gates unlatched. The old black man, who'd come to them from a Kentucky breeding farm, had been around horses all his life and helped with the retraining of the rescue horses. He took his responsibilities seriously.

"He must have jumped the fence," her father said. "I should have known better than to leave him in the paddock, especially with some of the mares in heat."

Leslie grimaced. No wonder her father was furious.

"You said you wanted to be responsible for this guy," Mr. D'Andrea said sternly. "From now on he goes in the barn at night. We have a free stall, but it looks like he's more than we bargained for. I'm going to have to consider gelding him."

"No. Can't we give him a little time to get used to the place?" Leslie pleaded. "He'll settle down."

14

She tried to lay a hand on the excited horse's silky, muscular neck and nearly got bitten for her efforts.

Her father shook his head. "I told you at the auction that stallions are too high-strung and unpredictable. There's no point in having one around unless you intend to breed him—and we definitely don't! His bloodlines are only mediocre anyway."

"They're not that bad! I mean, he's got some Northern Dancer and Princequillo—"

"Way back in his family tree. You wouldn't be hatching up any ideas of breeding him ourselves, would you?"

Leslie flushed for a second. "I guess I did think of it. I mean, you train some incredible racehorses. Why couldn't we breed a couple of our own?"

"This horse is unproven. He never won a race—and he ended up being auctioned for horse meat with a bunch of third-class claimers."

"Because the owners of the string went bankrupt!" Leslie quickly put in.

"That doesn't recommend him as good breeding stock." Her father frowned at her stubbornness and handed her Battlecry's lead shank. "Get this animal his breakfast, then come out to the oval. You've got horses to work this morning."

Leslie nodded meekly, and her father strode up the drive toward the stable building where his horses in training were housed. Opposite the stable was the half-mile training oval. Both were surrounded by thirty acres of fenced paddock and pasture, although in late February, the grass was a

15

dull brown. The D'Andrea farm was one of the few open spaces left amid sprawling housing developments in that section of Long Island.

Battlecry jerked at the lead shank and nudged Leslie sharply with his nose. "Yes, I know. You're hungry," she said. "I'll get you your breakfast, but doggone it, you've got to start behaving! I had to twist my father's arm to buy you. He didn't want to, you know, and he isn't going to put up with any more of your badness."

Battlecry tossed his head impatiently and pranced up the stable aisle as Leslie led him to a big box stall at the end. He went in willingly, though, knowing from experience that food was coming. "Your new home, until you start behaving yourself," Leslie told him. Edwin had already filled the hay net and water bucket. Leslie went to the feed room, measured out a portion of grain into a feed bucket, and carried it back to the stall. Battlecry had his head over the door, waiting. He nearly knocked the feed from Leslie's hands as she entered his stall.

"Hey!" she said sharply. "The first thing you're going to learn is some manners, big boy. You get back and wait until I get this feed where it belongs."

The stallion stopped his pushing, but he seemed puzzled that he was actually obeying her. Others might have been wary of his size and notorious temperament, but Leslie wasn't going to let him intimidate her, even if she only stood five foot three and weighed a hundred and ten pounds to his thousand plus.

She filled his feed bin, stepped back, and nodded at the horse. "Good boy. Okay, go get it."

With a superior snort, Battlecry went to his feed. Leslie bolted the stall door and left the stable for the training oval.

As Leslie approached the track across the tree-lined stable yard, she saw her father standing near the rail. Jeremy was holding the reins of two horses. Another horse was being worked on the track by their part-time exercise rider, Tim Donaldson. Tim and Leslie shared the riding.

Mr. D'Andrea clicked his stopwatch as the horse and Tim passed. "Good," he said under his breath, then he saw his daughter. "The filly Tim's on looks good," he said. "She's all set to go to Aqueduct next weekend. Take Maestro out first—just a light work. Half-mile gallop, two-furlong breeze."

Leslie nodded and walked over to take the reins of a bay gelding from Jeremy. "Get that stallion settled?" Jeremy asked with a twinkle in his blue eyes. "Your dad wasn't too happy this morning."

"I could tell."

"That monster nearly kicked Edwin when he caught him."

Leslie swung into Maestro's saddle. "What do you expect? He was having a good time."

"Too much horse to have around here."

Leslie didn't answer as she rode toward the ring. She carefully followed her father's instructions as she moved Maestro out onto the oval, but her mind was on Battlecry, his behavior, and her father's anger. She had to figure out some way to calm the big horse down—get through to him and let him know she was a friend he could trust. It would be a real challenge, but that only made Leslie want to try harder. She could just picture what Battlecry could do if he put his heart and mind to it. He was one of the most promising horses Leslie had ever seen.

She finished Maestro's workout, then took out one of her father's old campaigners, Top Drawer. He needed only a light gallop before being shipped to Aqueduct.

Mr. D'Andrea looked satisfied as she rode off and dismounted.

"I thought I'd give the stallion a little exercise on the oval," Leslie said lightly. "Maybe that'll calm him down."

Her father instantly scowled. "Think that's smart after yesterday? You'd be better off walking him on the lead shank."

"He'll need the exercise if he's going to be in the stall instead of the paddock. And you know I can handle high-strung horses."

"That horse isn't just high-strung—he could be spooky." Mr. D'Andrea screwed up his mouth thoughtfully. "Well, if you're careful. But keep him in hand!"

"Promise, Dad! Just some slow, easy stuff." Leslie tried to hide her grin of success. One great thing about her father, Leslie thought, was that he trusted completely in her skill on horseback. Of course, he'd taught her himself, and he could ride as well as any of the jockeys he put on his horses.

A half hour later Leslie led the saddled and bridled Battlecry out of the barn. The stallion had been showing every bit of his high-minded nature as Leslie had tacked him up. He had twice refused the bit. Then he had danced in a half circle as Leslie tried to get the saddle in place and tighten the girth. When she was finally successful, he flattened his ears and pawed the ground.

"Cut it out," Leslie told him firmly. "You're not impressing anybody. You've gotten away with stuff for too long. I know it's just a big act."

The horse whuffed indignantly, but pricked his ears forward again.

"That's better," Leslie told him with a pat and a smile. "You'd almost think you'd *rather* be stallion steak on somebody's table."

As she turned to lead the stallion off, a red jeep came roaring up the drive, sending a cloud of dust into the air behind it. It screeched to a stop, and Leslie's two best friends, Kim and Gabby, jumped out. Kim was tall, slim, and athletic, with pretty features and bone-straight black hair. Gabby, on the other hand, was short and freckled with a mop of strawberry-blond curls. The three of them had done everything together since their first day in kindergarten. Kim had just turned sixteen in January, and had promptly gotten her driver's license and the use of her father's jeep. Leslie and Gabby still had months to wait.

"So this is the new stallion," Gabby said. "He's gorgeous—I can't believe they were going to sell him to a butcher."

Kim grimaced. "The whole idea of sending Thoroughbreds to a slaughterhouse is disgusting. What kind of people would actually eat *horse*-meat?"

"They don't seem to mind in Europe," Leslie said sourly. "That's where the meat usually ends up. Or in dog food here."

"It's a good thing there are people like your parents," Kim said. "This guy looks really great."

"And he's in trouble already," Leslie said, then described Battlecry's nighttime adventure.

"Have you ridden him yet?" Gabby asked. "I'll bet he's a handful."

"I jogged him around the paddock yesterday, and yeah, he is a handful. He nearly threw me, and fought every inch of the way, but he's got incredible movements. I can't figure out why he never did well at the track."

Kim arched a black eyebrow. "Maybe because he likes to throw riders and give them a hard time?"

"I'm taking him out on the oval now. Come and watch."

Gabby eyed Battlecry nervously as he suddenly danced around Leslie. "You sure you want to do that?"

"He's got to unlearn his bad habits sometime." Leslie didn't add that she was dying to see what Battlecry could do on the track. "Besides, I think he's going to turn out to be a big baby underneath. He just likes to show off."

"Well, if you don't break a leg, you can come to town with us afterward," Gabby said. "A couple of the guys are meeting us at the mall, and Kim and I want to buy some jeans."

"Great."

"Maybe you ought to just work him on a longe line for a while," Kim said when they all reached the oval.

Leslie gave Kim a surprised look. Kim was a superb and fearless rider. She owned one of the D'Andreas's reconditioned Thoroughbreds and kept him at a nearby stable, where she was training him for show jumping. "You've never been afraid of any horse!"

"I can tell he's more than I've ever handled," Kim said bluntly.

"He'll be okay when he learns who's boss," Leslie answered. "You'll see."

But Battlecry flung up his head, skittered, and eyed Leslie menacingly as she tried to mount him outside the ring. "Hold his head," she said to Kim as she grabbed the reins and a chunk of mane in her left hand and lifted her left foot toward the stirrup. It took Leslie a couple of hops before she could get her foot in the stirrup iron and swing her right leg over the saddle of the prancing animal.

21

Gabby stood silently watching. She rode too, but strictly for fun. She'd never had the competitive courage of Leslie and Kim. "You'd better not let him get his head," she warned, shaking her red mop of hair.

"I don't intend to," Leslie said firmly. She noticed her father come out of the training stable to stand beside her friends. Then she concentrated all her attention on the horse. Battlecry hadn't tried to throw her yet, as he'd done the day before, but she could feel the tension building in his muscles, like a spring stretched to the snapping point. Leslie settled deep in the English saddle and tightened her grip on the reins. Then she quickly but gently urged Battlecry forward through the gap onto the track.

Battlecry had seen the oval before, but Leslie knew that didn't mean he'd do what she expected. Although he had only walked a few yards up the track, he was already thrusting his head forward against the pressure of the reins. Leslie decided the wise approach was to let him use up some of his excess energy before he exploded in a series of bucks. Gradually, she let Battlecry out into a trot. He instantly strode out, demonstrating his beautiful gait. "Good boy," Leslie said softly. "Let's just keep it nice and easy."

Battlecry flicked back his ears, listening, but Leslie wasn't deceived into thinking that she now had a perfectly amiable horse beneath her. She needed all her muscle power to keep the stallion at a trot, and already she could feel the strain in her forearms and shoulders.

They circled the half-mile oval. Leslie looked at nothing but the harrowed dirt ahead, her senses tuned to the stallion as she waited for any change in his mood or movements. Her goal was to teach him to cooperate through firm gentleness; that was the way her father trained his horses. There was never any rough handling in his stable.

They circled the oval again. Battlecry's long strides, even at a trot, seemed to eat up the distance, but Leslie was gradually growing more confident.

"You're doing great, big boy," she praised softly. "Keep this up, and I think tomorrow we can try a canter."

The words were no sooner out of her mouth than the stallion bolted. In one fraction of a second, he gathered his powerful muscles, thrust his head forward, pulled the reins through Leslie's fingers, and was off at a full gallop! Leslie reacted instantly from long practice. She immediately sat back in the saddle, throwing her weight as far from the stallion's withers as possible without losing her balance. Her arms strained to draw back on the reins, but she knew she was no match for the headstrong horse. The best she could do for the next few seconds was to ride him out and try to exert enough control to prevent disaster.

Leslie's brain was clicking so quickly she wasn't even aware of her individual thoughts. She had to keep him from bolting through the rail—keep him circling the oval until he began to listen or had worn himself out. Her ears echoed with the rhythm of his pounding hooves and snorted breaths. Part of her mind was also registering their speed. They were flying! Battlecry was showing every one of his Thoroughbred genes. Unfortunately, he was also proving himself to be exactly as dangerous and unpredictable as his former trainer had warned!

Somehow, Leslie managed to keep the stallion to the center of the oval track. They flew around once, twice—then, from the corner of her eye, she saw her father riding one of his exercise ponies bareback through the gap. He was going to head them off. She just prayed that Battlecry didn't rebel at the interference and swerve out over the rail.

"Easy, boy, easy!" she called, trying to distract him. "Let's slow it down. You don't want to hurt yourself—or me." For an instant the stallion's ears flicked back. It was just time enough for her father to get the trained pony in position and angle toward them. In that second Leslie pulled the reins back, and her father leaned over and grabbed the stallion's bridle. For another dozen yards they half galloped, half cantered up the track, Battlecry fighting the hold on his bridle and reins. Then, with a snort, he seemed to give in. He slowed to a trot, angrily tossing his magnificent head.

Leslie dragged a much needed breath into her lungs. Her arms were shaking from the effort of

24

holding the horse. She looked over at her father. "Thanks," she gasped. "It happened so fast."

Surprisingly her father didn't look angry—more worried. "It was that backfire," he said.

"What backfire?"

"You didn't hear it?" Mr. D'Andrea let out his own breath. "Battlecry sure did."

At this news, Leslie felt a rush of relief. It hadn't been the stallion's fault after all. It wasn't his crazy-headed nature that had set him off.

"I'm just glad I came back to watch and that Danny was in the next paddock." He glanced down at the pinto exercise pony. In stature, Danny wasn't a pony at all; he stood nearly as tall as Battlecry and was much bigger boned, but traditionally exercise and escort horses were called ponies.

As they rode the two horses off the oval, Leslie saw that a small crowd had gathered. Jeremy and Nick Bates, a trainer friend of her father's, were standing with Kim and Gabby. Gabby's face was so white that her freckles stood out in stark contrast. Kim was staring at Battlecry with wide, disbelieving eyes.

"Well, that was something you don't see every day," Nick said to Leslie as she dismounted shakily and flipped the reins over Battlecry's head. As usual Nick wore a battered tweed sports jacket over his solid frame, although his black hair was neatly brushed. "You all right?" he asked.

Leslie nodded, but her legs felt like jelly. She noticed Nick had his stopwatch in his hand.

"Couldn't resist," he said, when he saw her glance at the watch. "He was flying. Spooked, of course, but you don't often see fractions like these! Beautiful action, too."

"I don't believe you, Nicky," Mr. D'Andrea snapped. "My daughter could have gotten killed, and you're clocking fractions!"

The dark-haired trainer ignored the irritation in Mr. D'Andrea's voice. "You given any thought to putting him back in training?"

"No, I haven't!" Mr. D'Andrea growled.

"Maybe you should. He's only five years old. From his size, it looks like he's only just grown into himself. He was probably as awkward as all get out as a two- or three-year-old. Not surprising he didn't perform well at the tracks."

Leslie was staring at Nick. Then she looked up at Battlecry, whose arrogant head was high. Despite the wild ride he'd just given her, he barely seemed winded or blown. Why hadn't she thought of that? It was a great idea! Battlecry could go back to racing! Why not? He should be given a second chance to prove himself—show what he could do with the right kind of handling.

Then she heard her father answer, "Forget it! He's had his chance at the track. I'm not going to be responsible for someone's getting killed just so he can have another try. No way! He's going to be gelded and sold on!"

3

Leslie jumped as someone abruptly sat down next to her on the mall bench. She looked up to see Adam Beauman's laughing face. He quickly sobered when he saw hers. "Boy, you look pretty bummed," he said, brushing his brown hair off his forehead. "What's wrong? Midterms? Relax. You still have a week and a half to cram."

"It's not that." Leslie shook her head. She and Adam had known each other for years and had slipped comfortably from friendship to dating. They spent a lot of time together, going to movies, hanging out at school, riding the D'Andreas's horses—and Leslie knew she could talk to Adam about almost anything.

Adam gave her a probing look. "So tell me."

Leslie did, describing everything that had happened with Battlecry that morning. She ended with, "I don't know why I care so much. But something tells me that this horse could really have a shot at being something great."

"It's not hopeless," Adam said when she was finished. "After what Nick suggested, maybe your father could still change his mind."

"Mmmm. He was pretty angry, though. Scared, I think, that I might have gotten hurt. *But*,"—Leslie paused and frowned—"I think my mother's on my side. Maybe the two of us can change Dad's mind."

Gabby and Kim came over, loaded down with shopping bags. "So what do you think of Leslie's stallion?" Gabby asked Adam.

"He sounds like something else, but I haven't seen him yet."

"Wait till you do," Gabby said with a wry smile. "That horse is wild! They should have called him Diablo instead of Battlecry, though that name describes him pretty well too."

Adam gave Gabby one of his lazy, crooked smiles. "Makes you nervous, huh?"

"You won't catch *me* riding him!"

Adam turned to Leslie. "How about if I stop by before I go to work tomorrow afternoon? I could take a look at ol' Battlecry. Is that okay?"

"Yeah, that'd be fine," she agreed. "And you can tell me what you think. You've seen a lot of horses on the farm."

"Hey, you guys!" a voice called from down the mall walkway. "You coming to get something to eat, or what?" Leslie and Adam jumped up and headed for Pizza Heaven, where the rest of their friends had already gathered.

"I heard the whole story from Nick," Mrs. D'Andrea said with a grin when Leslie talked to her mother that night before dinner. "Your father's being stubborn, and you want me to help try to change his mind, right?"

"Yes," Leslie answered. Her mother understood her eerily well. Not only did the two of them look alike—both silver blonds with blue eyes—but they thought alike. At least they did some of the time. "I think Battlecry's good enough for the track, Mom, and I'd work him."

"Okay, go ahead and talk to Dad at dinner," her mother answered. "I think that horse has potential too. I'll back you up."

"Thanks," Leslie said with a smile.

But she waited until her father was nearly finished with his meal and was looking content before she brought up Battlecry's training. He instantly shook his head. "Look, I'm already training twenty horses. Half of them look promising. I'll be busy at the track with them all summer. And the odds are completely against that stallion turning around and making a decent racehorse."

"But look at how he ran today! Won't you even think about it?" Leslie asked. "I'll do most of the work. I do know something about training." Which she did. As an only child, Leslie had grown up knowing that she could step into her father's shoes and take over the training when he was ready to retire, if that was what she wanted.

"He's a beautiful animal, Phil," Mrs. D'Andrea said. "Ten notches better than the rest of the rescue horses. What else are we going to do with him?"

"He didn't seem to have any trouble jumping the paddock fence. Gelded, he'd make a good jump horse for one of the riders around here."

"Battlecry's better than a local show-jump horse!" Leslie protested. "Maybe he'd make a good three-day eventer, but we don't have too many top-notch riders coming to us for horses."

Her mother gave her a warning look, then spoke calmly to her husband. "Nick was impressed with the stallion, and I know you respect his opinion."

"But Hawkins couldn't get anything out of him. Dead last in every one of his races—when he actually got in the race. Most of the time he acted up so badly at the gate that he was scratched."

"Maybe he just needed more time to mature and was pushed too hard early on," Mrs. D'Andrea reasoned.

"He's five, and he didn't set a hoof on the track until he was three." Mr. D'Andrea ladled some salad onto his plate.

Leslie, with difficulty, held her tongue and let her mother continue. "Some horses are still immature at three," Mrs. D'Andrea argued. "And it wouldn't really cost us anything to put him back in training, try him in a few small races if he comes along . . ."

"It would cost my time," Mr. D'Andrea said.

"So let Leslie take him on."

"I'd like to try, Dad."

"And if he doesn't work out," Mrs. D'Andrea added, "we can always go back to plan A."

Mr. D'Andrea groaned and ran his fingers through his tawny hair. "You two are ganging up on me again. Geez, women! Okay, I'll think about it."

When he looked down again at his plate, Leslie and her mother exchanged a subtle smile.

As soon as Leslie got home from school the next afternoon, she changed into work jeans, boots, and a heavy sweater and went out to the barn. After being in his stall all day, Battlecry would need some exercise in the paddock. Adam would be coming over too, and Leslie wanted him to see Battle out of the stall and moving around in the open air. Only then would he really be able to appreciate the big stallion's action and form. Her father had said nothing to her about Battle that morning when she'd worked the horses before school. He had other things on his mind, she knew, with several horses to get ready for races at Aqueduct that week. She wasn't about to push him.

Just as she was entering the barn, Adam puttered up the drive on his moped and parked under a nearby leafless tree. Leslie walked over with a smile. "Perfect timing," she said. "I was just going to take him out. Come on."

Together they entered the stable. They were barely through the door when Leslie heard a tremendous pounding noise, then the shrill cry of a horse. "Oh no," she moaned to Adam. The pounding sounded suspiciously like iron-shod hooves on a wooden stall side.

"Battlecry?" Adam asked.

"That's what I'm afraid of." She set off down the stable aisle at a jog, with Adam right behind. The shrill cries continued, and outside Battlecry's stall she saw an angry Jeremy and a worried Edwin.

"This is the second time we've tried to take him outside. He won't let me near him! You can sort him out," Jeremy said as soon as he saw her. "I'm not going in that stall!"

"He's crazy today," Edwin agreed. His kind, weathered face was creased with concern. "Doesn't like being in the stall. Fella like him needs to be out." Edwin had a special rapport with horses. Leslie sometimes thought he could read their minds, and he certainly seemed to be right about Battlecry.

"Easy, easy, boy," she called over the stall door. Battlecry was pacing the roomy box. He paused to lash out with one hind leg at the near wall, then gave another angry cry. "I know, I know, boy," Leslie soothed, "you just want to get out for a while. That's why I'm here. Just calm down now." She reached for the stallion's lead shank hanging

32

outside the stall and muttered to Jeremy, "Grab another shank. It's going to take two of us to get him out to the paddock. Adam, you'd better stay clear." Adam moved off toward the exit door.

Jeremy was backing away too. "I'm not going near him when he's in this kind of mood," he said. "Edwin's better with him anyway."

"Chicken," Leslie taunted.

"But a chicken without any broken bones," Jeremy shot back.

Battlecry saw the lead in Leslie's hand and knew what it meant. He immediately pranced to the stall door, head up, snorting. Edwin got another shank and walked up beside Leslie. "We'll clip both sides of his halter before I open the stall door," Edwin suggested. "Main thing'll be to keep him from rearing, coming down the aisle."

Leslie nodded and murmured, "Okay, boy, you're going out. Easy now," she added as she took his halter and quickly snapped the lead to the right side. Edwin did the same to the left, then moved clear of the path of the door as he swung it back. Battlecry exploded forward into the aisle, but they were prepared. Their hands were tight on the lead shanks, and they immediately started moving forward, one at either side of Battlecry's head. It took all their strength to keep the big horse from bolting forward on his own. He resented the restraint of the leads and tried to throw up his head.

"No nonsense now," Leslie said through gritted teeth as the three quickly moved toward the stable door. It was hard to tell who was leading whom, but within seconds they were outside. Battlecry instantly let out a piercing whinny. Adam had already opened the gate of the paddock behind the barn and was standing ready to close it after the horse. Leslie and Edwin led Battlecry through. "Ready?" Leslie breathed to Edwin. "One, two, three." Simultaneously they unclipped the leads and stepped back. Battlecry thundered forward down the length of the grassy paddock, kicking out his heels in ecstasy. Leslie and Edwin made their way to the fence and climbed over. But Battlecry had what he wanted—fresh air and running room. He ignored the humans as he raced happily around the paddock. For a worried second, Leslie thought the stallion might decide to go flying over the rear fence.

Edwin saw her expression. "The mares are way out in the back paddock," he said.

"Whew! I didn't even think of them when we put him in here."

She, Edwin, and Adam watched as Battlecry circled the paddock at a gallop. His silky black mane and tail flew out behind him.

"Some horse," Edwin said. "Haven't seen anything like him in years, since I worked the big breeding farms in Kentucky."

Leslie turned and grinned at Adam. "So, what do you think?"

"Wild! You're seriously thinking of training him?"

"He's more high-strung than usual today because he hasn't had any exercise. But isn't he beautiful?"

Jeremy had come up behind them and made a snorting noise. "Sure."

"Come on, Jeremy," Adam said. "You've been around racehorses most of your life. You must have seen wild ones like him before."

"Not as bad as him. He's just plain nasty. Right, Edwin?"

The old man rubbed a hand over his nearly white hair. "Naw. Not nasty. High spirits. Knows he's something special. This fella just needs the right handling. Firm but gentle."

"All right, Edwin!" Leslie cried. "At least you're on my side."

Edwin smiled slowly. "That I am. I see lots of potential here—if we can get through to him."

"How would you guys know?" Jeremy grumbled. "Neither of you even heard of this colt till Leslie saw him at the auction."

"But I've been on the backside of the track enough to know that Hawkins tends to muscle his animals around if they don't behave," Leslie said. "And Edwin knows more about training horses than you do."

Jeremy shrugged. "Maybe Hawkins needed to muscle this one around. Personally, I'm keeping as much distance between me and that horse as I can."

Battlecry had gotten rid of the worst of his high

spirits and had settled down to graze on the browned grass, though he stayed at the far end of the paddock. Every so often he lifted his head and stared defiantly at the four humans as if to say, "Don't even *think* about trying to catch me."

"I'll say one thing," Adam mused. "He's got incredible movements. If he set his mind to it, I can see how he'd burn up a racetrack."

"The problem," Jeremy grunted, "is getting him to set his mind to it."

"I'll fix that," Leslie said.

Jeremy laughed. "Keep dreaming. I just hope your dad's got enough sense not to give in to you this time."

Leslie took a playful swipe at him. "You trying to say I'm a spoiled brat?"

Jeremy ducked. "Well, not a brat . . . exactly."

"Thanks!"

Jeremy dusted off his jeans. "I've got work to do."

"I'll be off too," Edwin agreed. "Call me when you want to bring him in."

Adam and Leslie stayed by the paddock until it was time for Adam to go to work at a local seafood restaurant, where he was a busboy.

"I hope your father says yes," he told Leslie, giving her a hug. "I'm with you. This guy might just be something special. But you be careful. See you at school tomorrow."

She flashed him a happy smile as he climbed on his moped. Three people were on her side—her mother, Edwin, and Adam. Things were looking up.

Just before dark Leslie decided to get Battlecry from the paddock by herself. His afternoon's exercise and freedom had calmed him, but she brought some carrots as a bribe, just in case, and carried the lead shank behind her back, out of his line of vision. He was grazing, but lifted his head when she approached.

"Hi there, fella," she called. "Look what I've got for you." She extended her hand with the carrots. Battlecry sniffed and eyed her, obviously undecided whether to bolt off or give in to the temptation of a treat. Leslie stepped slowly toward him, watching as his ears flicked back, then forward. As she drew near, his muscles twitched under his gleaming black coat, then he thrust out his head and lipped up one of the carrots. In a flash, Leslie brought the lead shank around and clipped it to Battlecry's halter. He whinnied indignantly at being tricked once again, but Leslie rewarded him with another carrot. As he munched, she rubbed her hand over his powerful neck. "You *can* be nice when you want to. Let's go back to the stall. Your supper's waiting." As she talked, she started leading him toward the gate. After only a mild show of protest, he followed.

She'd planned ahead and had already filled the feed bucket in his stall. Battlecry went toward it eagerly after Leslie led him inside and unclipped the lead. Then she reached in the tack box outside the stall for some brushes and groomed him as he ate. Battlecry needed to grow accustomed to her voice and touch—and to learn that she wasn't afraid of him. Obviously, someone who'd handled him in the past *had* been afraid. The stallion had taken full advantage.

Leslie gently ran the brush over Battlecry's strong back. His muscles rippled in response. "I think it's time we started to be good friends," she said softly. "And friends don't fight each other." Battlecry stomped his foot. There was definitely a glint of mischief in his eyes. "Or kick out the stall, or bite," Leslie continued dryly. "I know you're high spirited—you're supposed to be. You just have to learn to behave a little better and stop doing things that get you in trouble. Nobody's going to take all your fun away." The stallion blew through his nose. "I mean it. I think you can do something fantastic on the track, but it's going to take some work to get you there. That'll be one way to get rid of your extra energy."

Leslie continued talking to the horse, letting him become familiar with her voice and using her tone to soothe. Edwin came by as he finished his evening rounds and smiled his approval. A few minutes later Leslie turned when she heard new footsteps outside the stall. Battlecry threw up his head and grunted in surprise.

Leslie's father stopped outside the door. "Trying to talk him down?" he said, looking the big horse over. "You've got your work cut out for you." He paused and continued studying Battlecry. "I have to admit he's got beautiful conformation—and speed when he wants to run." Mr. D'Andrea shook his head thoughtfully. "Nick just called me. He was looking over this guy's family tree. Seems there's both speed and stamina in his line, and Nick tells me that the majority of the offspring of this cross are late bloomers. He offered to buy him from us—"

"Nick did? But you're not going to sell him!" Leslie cried.

"He offered a darn good price, considering."

Leslie's heart plunged to her feet. "No, Dad! You said—"

"I need to think about it. Frankly, I feel you're taking on too much trying to undo his bad attitude and habits—whether he goes back to racing or you start schooling him as a jumper. He's just a bad character. I wouldn't waste my time on a horse like him unless he was winning some big races— and even that would be a gamble. An offer like Nick's doesn't come along every day. I'd be crazy to turn it down."

"Battle's only been here two days," Leslie pleaded. "He hasn't had a chance to get to know me. He's the best horse we've ever gotten from the auction. Even you said he didn't belong there."

"That was before I got a taste of his personality."

"But Dad, it's just so important to me," Leslie continued. "I can't explain it, but I've never felt like this about the other horses we rescued. He's got something special. I know that once he settles down and starts concentrating, he could be incredible."

"It sounds to me like you're out to prove something," her father said. "You'd be leaving yourself open for a big disappointment."

"But Nick must think there's something special too, or he wouldn't be interested in buying him!"

"Look, Nick needs a new project. He's getting bored, and he'd be the first to admit he's taking a big chance. But he can afford to take the chance."

"I'm the one who found him at the auction," Leslie said desperately. "I can't give him up already. Can't I at least *try* to retrain him?"

"Les, he'll have a good home if he goes to Nick. Nick never mistreats an animal."

"Battlecry's mine!" Leslie was close to tears. She knew Battle wasn't really her property—he was owned by the farm. They all shared the responsibilities of caring for the rescue horses, but of course her parents paid the bills and made the major decisions.

Her father was frowning, deep in thought. Then he sighed. "I'll see," he said finally. "I have to decide what's best in the long run." He laid a hand on Leslie's shoulder. "Honey, I'm not trying to be mean—you know that. But we don't make any money on the rescue operation. We're only involved because we hate to see a good horse put down. It's really contributions that keep that part of the farm going. This stallion isn't going to be easy to resell. When a decent offer comes along, I have to consider it, for the good of the whole farm."

Leslie nodded mutely, feeling both angry and very sad. She wished Nick had never been at the farm that day to see Battlecry run.

4

Leslie called Kim after dinner that night. "My father told me Nick wants to buy Battlecry," she said miserably.

"Nick really wants him?" Kim asked in surprise.

Leslie plucked angrily at the fringe on her bed-spread. "You don't have to sound like that. Battle isn't exactly a swaybacked nag!"

"I didn't mean it that way. I was just thinking of his reputation and temper. Nick must have liked how he ran yesterday."

"He did. And he's looked into Battle's blood-lines and liked what he saw there, too."

"Can't you get your dad to put him back in training himself—or let you?"

"I've been trying. But he doesn't believe Battle will change."

"I guess I can see why he thinks that. He was

pretty shook up when Battlecry spooked with you."

"But there was a reason for him to spook. If Nick thinks he can turn him around, then I know I can too."

"Well, I hope it works out okay. I know how you feel. I wouldn't want to lose Desert Sheik, either," Kim said, naming her own horse. "Listen, have you done your geometry homework yet?"

"I just finished it."

"How did you do the last problem? I can't figure it out at all."

Adam was waiting at Leslie's locker the next morning. He'd worked too late for her to call him the night before. "So what's the latest news?" he asked.

"Bad news," she said, hanging up her jacket. As she explained what had happened, Gabby and Kim joined them.

"That's too bad. I'm sorry," Adam said. "I wanted to see you get a chance to retrain him too."

"But why do you like *this* horse so much?" Gabby asked Leslie. "I mean, you've retrained tons of horses. You don't get upset when they're sold."

"Well, I do sometimes. But Battlecry is different. He's just so much better than any of the horses we've gotten from the auctions. You saw him. He has perfect conformation, and he's got talent. From the minute I saw him, I knew he was special. I almost felt like he was asking me personally to save him. I know it sounds dumb . . ."

"Not to me," Adam said quickly.

Kim nodded in understanding. "That's kind of how I felt when I saw Desert Sheik. I just knew we'd be perfect together on the jump course."

"At least your family is good friends with Nick," Gabby said. "If he does buy Battle, it's not like you wouldn't see him again."

"Yeah," Leslie said. But she knew it wouldn't be the same.

"You're still coming with me to the basketball game after school, aren't you?" Adam asked.

"Sure!" Leslie said. "I put Battle out in the paddock before I left for school, so he'll be fine. And this is probably the only game of the season we're going to win. I mean, St. Andrews is *really* bad."

"They'd have to be, to lose to us," Gabby said with a giggle.

The game was great. Adam and Leslie cheered until they were hoarse as the home team of George Watkins High demolished St. Andrews. "It's nice to win for a change," Leslie said, laughing as they climbed down the bleachers. "You all want to get some burgers?"

"Yup," Kim answered. "I've got the jeep today."

"I just have to get home in time to bring Battle in. I don't want to give my father anything else to be mad about." For the first time in hours, Leslie was reminded of her problem. It brought her spirits down with a crash. Adam saw her expression

44

and reached over to take her hand as they left the gym. "Your dad will decide to keep him," he said.

Yet for the next twenty-four hours, Leslie was left on pins and needles. Her father didn't say anything about his decision, and she didn't have the courage to bring up the subject. Wednesday night at dinner he had other worries. Top Drawer was off his feed.

"If he doesn't pick up tomorrow," Mr. D'Andrea said, "I'll have to scratch him from Sunday's race. I hate to, because it's a perfect spot for him, and he's got a good shot at winning."

"You still have the filly," Mrs. D'Andrea said.

"Yeah," he agreed. "We'll give her a good gallop in the morning," he said matter-of-factly to Leslie. "Get her on her toes."

"Sure," Leslie said quietly.

As soon as the meal was finished, Leslie cleared the table, put the dishes in the dishwasher, and went out to the barn. She had almost no homework that night, so she could spend some extra time with Battlecry. It might be one of the last chances she had.

To Leslie's amazement, Battlecry nickered when he saw her approach his stall.

"You mean you're actually glad to see me?" Leslie grinned as she let herself into the stall. But would it even matter if her father decided to go ahead and sell the stallion?

Battlecry eyed her. He obviously wasn't ready to

45

get too friendly yet, but he stood quietly as she rubbed her hand down his silky neck and scratched behind his ears. He seemed to especially like the ear scratching. Leslie smiled when he let out a long, relaxed breath.

"You know, if you'd start trusting people instead of acting up, you just might make something of yourself. I don't think you'd mind showing off in the winner's circle."

Battlecry grunted.

"Don't give me that. You'd love it," Leslie scolded gently. "But it looks like I might not be the one to get you there. If Nick buys you, you'll be going to his stable instead. He's a great trainer and a nice guy, but you're just starting to get used to it here . . . getting used to me."

Leslie felt her eyes sting and quickly blinked. "You know I'll miss you. Maybe my father doesn't believe in you, but I think you could be the best horse he's ever had in his stables!"

Battlecry suddenly flung up his head and tensed his muscles. He gave an uneasy snort. Leslie went to the stall door and saw her father walking up the barn aisle. She swallowed hard. From the expression on his face, she could tell that he'd made a decision—and she didn't think it was going to make her happy.

Mr. D'Andrea leaned his arms on the stall half door. His eyes rested on Battlecry, who was pawing the bedding of his stall with his nostrils flared.

"Cut it out," Leslie whispered automatically to the horse, but she was watching her father.

He turned to her. "Well, I've just had a long talk with your mother, and I called Nick to talk to him, too. Your mother wants me to give you a shot at retraining the horse. She reminded me that we didn't exactly pay a fortune for this guy. If you could manage to turn him around, and he won a race or two, she thinks he could pay for what we invested in him." Her father pursed his lips. He didn't look convinced of that possibility himself. "Nick feels the same," he added with a frown. "He said he only made the offer because he's intrigued enough with the stallion to want to give him another chance. He didn't think I was going to do that." He paused. "I wasn't. It's against my better judgment. But if it's so important to you, I'll listen to opposing advice and give it a shot."

Leslie felt her heart leap, but her father wasn't finished yet.

"I'll give him two months. Next week is the first of March, so you'll have until the end of April. If he's still showing no signs of being ready to go back to the track, I'm going to geld him and have Edwin or your mother start schooling him for jumps. Fair enough?"

Leslie swallowed again. "Yes. That's fair. Thank you, Dad."

"It's going to be hard work. Don't get your hopes up too high," he warned. "There are no guarantees. I've dealt with guys like this one

47

before. It can be worth the effort, but it can be one big disappointment, too."

"I don't mind working hard." Leslie could hardly contain her happiness.

"I've put him in the training schedule as of tomorrow. He'll be your responsibility. I'll give you a hand occasionally and advice, but it's up to you. We'll see how it goes."

Before Leslie could say another word, her father walked off. Eyes shining, Leslie turned to Battlecry and in her excitement almost hugged him. Fortunately, she stopped herself in time. The stallion would never have put up with that much intimacy yet. Leslie laid a hand on his shoulder instead. "You're going to have a second chance, you big monster. Just don't blow it this time!"

Battlecry studied her with a keenly intelligent eye, thrust his sculpted nose in the air, and then went back to his feed.

Over the next days, Leslie put all her excess time and energy into Battlecry's training. Edwin volunteered his advice and suggested they start by working Battle on the longe line, circling him at a walk, trot, and canter. The exercise would smooth his gaits and reinforce his response to their commands.

"So you think he's worth the effort too," Leslie said to the old man.

"Yeah, Les, I do."

Of course, Battle had gone through all this preliminary training before. It wasn't new to him, but he couldn't resist trying to impose his own will. He taxed Leslie and Edwin's combined patience to the limit before finally settling down and doing what was asked of him.

Leslie saw Jeremy watching from outside the paddock. He shook his head at them and called, "Lost cause!"

"Wait and see!" Leslie yelled back.

When Battlecry *did* do what he was supposed to, Leslie was quick to reward him.

"That's what this fella's been missing," Edwin told her. "Praise. All he's heard lately are people yelling at him. You keep praising him when he does a good job, and he'll start wanting to please you. You'll see a difference."

Leslie thought so too. Unfortunately, praise wasn't always warranted. It totally depended on Battle's mood for the day. A week into his training, Leslie decided to take him back out to the oval to walk and trot him under tack. It meant getting up a half hour earlier, since she had all her regular horses to work, plus Battlecry, and still had to be finished in time to get ready for school. The loss of sleep was worth it to her if it would speed up Battlecry's progress, but she never knew whether he would try to toss her or would angelically follow her commands.

For three days in a row, Battle behaved like a dream. Leslie felt confident when she took him out of the stall the next morning. He seemed in high spirits when she tacked him up, but despite the glint of mischief in his eye, he wasn't really misbehaving. She was relaxed in the saddle as she rode Battle through the gap onto the track. "We going to have a good work this morning, like we did yesterday?" she asked as she urged him up the track.

Battle flicked back his ears and snorted softly. They circled the track once at a walk. "Okay, let's pick it up a little," Leslie said. She tightened her legs on his girth, indicating she wanted a trot. Battlecry danced sideways, and in the next instant had gathered his muscles and did three bucking leaps up the track.

Before Leslie knew what had happened, she was on her back in the dirt and Battlecry was merrily trotting up the track, shaking his elegant head in pure glee.

Leslie rose quickly, caught her breath, dusted herself off, and shook her fist at him. There was no point in yelling. As Edwin had said, Battle had heard too much yelling from people already. Fortunately, aside from a few bruises, she wasn't hurt. But she *was* furious—with herself as much as the horse. She'd been too relaxed. She hadn't been prepared.

Leslie waited until her father, mounted on Danny, caught the stallion and brought him back around the track. Battle was looking incredibly pleased with himself. He cocked his head and almost seemed to be laughing at her. Leslie gritted her teeth and immediately remounted, determined not to lose the upper hand this time. Yet as she started him up the track again, she suddenly had a perfectly well-mannered horse beneath her. It was as if Battle had decided he'd made his point and could afford to behave himself now. "You *are* a monster," she muttered to him. "Don't expect to catch me unprepared again!"

Battle gave a confident shake of his head.

After that Leslie stuck like glue to his saddle. Whenever Battle tried to toss her, she grabbed fistfuls of his mane and sank her heels deep in the stirrups. "You're not getting rid of me that easily. I'm not giving up! You're going to start behaving and listening—and you're going to race again! Whether you like it or not!"

Gradually Battlecry seemed to get the message that Leslie's determination was greater than anything he'd encountered in the past. His scare tactics didn't work with her, although he didn't stop testing her—waiting for the one instant when she was unprepared.

Leslie's father watched the battle of wills and sometimes shook his head. "Well, you'd both get top grades for stubbornness. It'll be interesting to see who wins the contest."

As the March days grew warmer and crocuses bloomed around the farmhouse, Leslie was pretty sure she was gaining ground. The stallion was forming a bond with her. Now his head came over his stall door as soon as he heard her voice, and he'd calmed down enough that she could get him in and out of his stall herself—something he wouldn't allow even Edwin to do without kicking up a fuss.

Yet by early April, there were times when Leslie wanted to sit down and cry in frustration.

"He was a real jerk this morning," she told Kim and Gabby at lunch on Thursday. A steady rain was streaming down the cafeteria windows near their table, matching Leslie's mood.

"When I came over to see him last week, he looked good," Kim said.

Leslie yawned, wondering how she was going to stay awake to take her history test next period. It had started to rain while she'd been working Battle, and she'd gotten so wet, she still felt chilled. "Yeah, but now I'm trying to work him up into some light gallops, and he's being such a creep—doing exactly what he did for his old trainer. He won't put anything into it—he either backs off the pace or tries to bolt with me. I just don't know what to do! My father's been giving me a couple of tips, but he looks pretty disgusted. Maybe he's right."

"You don't mean that!" Kim said with surprise.

"No . . ." Leslie sighed. "I guess I'm just tired, but I'm sure glad tomorrow's Friday."

Kim leaned forward. "Come with me to the horse show on Saturday. You need to take a day off, and you can see how well Desert is coming along. I got up the courage and entered us in the advanced class this time.''

Leslie's face brightened. ''You did? That's great. Sure, I'll come. Adam's not working Saturday. Could I ask him, too?''

''Sure! I need a cheering section.''

Suddenly Leslie felt a little less exhausted. ''I definitely am ready to take a day off.''

5

"This horse is going to be the death of one of us!" Mr. D'Andrea looked like he was ready to pull out his hair as he strode angrily across the grass toward the training oval entrance. The mid-April sun was just peeking over the newly leafed treetops around the ring. Leslie was so frustrated, she felt like she'd been up for hours. She rode Battlecry toward her father. The stallion skittered over the dew-covered grass, tossing his head. In the past two weeks, Battlecry had made almost no progress.

"I can see why Hawkins washed his hands of him," Mr. D'Andrea continued. "He's impossible!" Despite himself, her father had been coaching Leslie. He couldn't be around the training oval without giving advice, especially now that Battlecry had progressed to the point of timed gallops. Leslie had begun to think that he was taking a real interest in Battlecry, but this morning he seemed at the end of his rope.

"Dad, I've tried everything," Leslie said, sighing. "But he does exactly the opposite of what I ask. As soon as I give him the signal to gallop, he backs right off the pace. I let him have all the rein he wants, and he still won't pick it up. But when he thinks I'm not paying attention, he tries to bolt. We could try a crop, but I think that would just make him worse."

"No, don't use any whips on him. I think part of his problem is that Hawkins was too quick to use the whip."

Leslie dismounted as her father held Battlecry's head. "He's still testing me," she said. "But once he finds out I can be just as stubborn as he is, he's bound to improve."

"And my hair may have turned gray by then!" Her father tightened his mouth and squinted thoughtfully as he looked the stallion over.

Leslie knew too well that her deadline for re-training Battlecry was rapidly coming up. Her father would stick to their bargain, and she was getting panicky. "I've been thinking of something else, Dad," she said. "Maybe if we gallop him with another horse, it will wake him up."

Mr. D'Andrea considered that for a moment, then nodded. "Okay, it's worth a try. It can't hurt."

Her father turned and motioned to Tim Donaldson, who was standing nearby with Jeremy and several other saddled horses. "Take Sunny out," he told Tim.

"Sure." The wiry young rider took the reins of the gray colt who was to be worked next and led the horse over.

"Work inside of Battlecry," Mr. D'Andrea instructed Tim, "but pace Sunny to stay even with him for the first quarter mile. Then let Sunny out a notch. Let's see if this terror will forget himself enough to try to keep up."

"Might help." Tim nodded. "You've never worked him with another horse before." He and Leslie each mounted and rode out onto the oval. Battlecry was instantly alert to the change of routine, snorting and eyeing the other colt. Leslie didn't want any fireworks, so she kept Battlecry several yards clear of Sunny and held the reins in a very firm grip. The two horses moved side by side up the track first at a trot, then a canter. Once they'd lapped the track, Leslie glanced over at Tim, who nodded. Simultaneously they gave the horses more rein. Sunny jumped forward into a gallop, but Battlecry refused to obey Leslie's signal —that is, until he saw the other horse getting away from him. Suddenly he let out an angry grunt and changed gaits so swiftly that he nearly unbalanced Leslie.

Battle pulled up to Sunny's side. The two horses matched strides as they rounded the turn at a steady, even gallop. Halfway down the backstretch, Tim let Sunny out another notch. The colt instantly increased his speed and quickly gained a length lead on Battlecry and Leslie.

Leslie could feel Battlecry's shudder of surprise. "Well, if you don't like it, go get him!" she cried as she gave the stallion rein and dropped lower over his withers.

To her amazement, Battlecry shot forward! In two strides, he was even again with Sunny, but now was the real test. Would he show the grit and determination to go to the front?

Leslie clucked in his ears and kneaded her hands along his neck. "Keep going, Battle! Beat him!"

Battlecry was already eyeing Sunny. He gathered his muscles and responded with a new burst of speed. They surged past Sunny and Tim, and Battlecry did it effortlessly!

Leslie gasped with delight. Grinning, Tim let Sunny out another notch. The horse moved up to challenge Battlecry again. Battlecry met the challenge, and now they had a real horse race on their hands!

Sunny edged up inside, but Battlecry wasn't about to lose his lead. He accelerated again, needing no more encouragement from Leslie. The big stallion was flying, fired by this new experience of being the best. His long strides ate up the ground. He and Leslie roared off the turn and down the stretch, and Battle showed no signs of tiring. Leslie glanced back and saw that they'd left Sunny and Tim in the dust!

When they swept past the half-mile marker, Leslie lifted her weight from Battlecry's neck and started pulling him up. For several nerve-racking moments he fought her, too exhilarated by the thrill of winning to stop. "Easy, Battle," Leslie called briskly. "You've done it! You beat him! Good boy!" The stallion slowly responded. "Good boy!" Leslie repeated. "I'm proud of you now!"

Battlecry clearly understood the tone in her voice. He tossed his sleek head and arched his neck. Leslie laughed with delight and firmly rubbed his neck. "See how great it feels doing what you're supposed to do?"

The big horse lifted his feet a little higher as Leslie turned him and trotted back toward her father.

"Well, well," Tim said as he rode up beside her. "I didn't think I'd see the day. And Sunny here is no slouch. You may make something out of the big nuisance yet."

"Correction," Leslie said breathlessly, "now I *know* we will! He just needed a taste of being in front. I don't think he's ever had it before now."

Her father was positively cheerful as he walked up to them. "Well, you monster," he said as he held Battle's head so Leslie could dismount, "you finally showed us what you could do. You keep on training like that, and you might make a liar out of me."

The stallion was basking in all the praise. His head was high, and he whuffed through his delicately flared nostrils. As Leslie dismounted, she saw Jeremy gaping from the sidelines. "So, what do you think now?" she called.

"I'm still not going in the stall with him," he said firmly. "And how do you know he'll keep training like that?"

"We don't know," Mr. D'Andrea said. "But I feel more optimistic than I did earlier this morning. Okay, cool him out," he added to Leslie. "Then you'd better make tracks for school. We're running late today."

"This is turning into more of a party than a training session," Mr. D'Andrea grumbled as Leslie, Kim, and Adam prepared to set out from the farm for a ride on the beach a week later. Kim had just ridden up the drive on her horse, Desert Sheik. Adam was in the saddle on one of the D'Andreas's reconditioned geldings, Romeo. Mr. D'Andrea was mounted on their exercise pony, Danny, and held a leading rein attached to Battlecry's bridle. Leslie swung up into his saddle, soothing the prancing horse with her voice. "Battle!" she scolded. "You stop trying to nip the other horses!"

They seemed to have found the magic trick in getting Battlecry to want to run. Once he'd discovered what it was like to be in front and kick dirt into another horse's face, he'd started putting his heart into it. And Leslie's praise after the two gallops he'd had that week had encouraged him even more. The black horse strutted like a peacock when she told him he'd done well. Yet the intense part of his retraining was just beginning. Not only would he need speed on the track, but he'd need stamina, too, which was why they'd come up with the idea of running him on the beach. Galloping on the sand would provide great exercise for his legs and lungs. Leslie knew her father wasn't entirely convinced the horse had turned over a new leaf. There was still a fear he'd go back to his old behavior. But she really felt optimistic now.

"You two stay behind us," Mr. D'Andrea said to Kim and Adam. "This'll be a new experience for the stallion, and it'll be better if he doesn't see any horses in front of him. All set?"

They nodded. Mr. D'Andrea started Danny off at a walk down their short, tree-lined drive. Leslie and Battlecry moved close beside them at the end of the leading rein. The horse was behaving nicely as they approached the overgrown hedge that shielded the farm from the road beyond. But once they passed through the wooden gates, the scenery changed completely. The opposite side of the street was lined with houses on manicured quarter-acre plots. Each house looked exactly the same except for the color of paint. Several cars sped by, and kids pedaled down the opposite sidewalk on bikes. Only the names of the many side streets—Burrell Farm Lane, Circle, and Prospect—gave any hint that the cluster of houses stood on what had once been a huge farm. Battlecry stopped in his tracks, startled by the change. "Easy," Leslie said.

"Just a few cars, and we'll be at the beach in a second."

Her father kept Danny to the outside and turned right along the still unpaved pathway that led along the front of the D'Andrea farm. After a moment's hesitation Battlecry followed, but he fidgeted uneasily, and Leslie was definitely glad her father had a firm grip on the lead shank. Two streets up they waited for a break in traffic, then crossed into a narrow, dead-end street. The houses along this street were older and surrounded by mature trees. The narrow road led to a back access to the public beach by way of a sandy path through scrub pine and dune grass. As they entered the path, Battlecry lifted his head and sniffed.

"Smell the salt?" Leslie smiled. "Wait till you see the beach."

The stallion nickered and tried to pull ahead, but Leslie held him back with the reins. They mounted a sandy rise, and then in front of them spread the wave-washed beach. The sun was just setting to the west, but it was a cool evening for late April, and the beach was almost deserted.

"Trot him down and let him get his feet wet," Mr. D'Andrea said. "I'll stay with you until he gets used to it, then you can jog him along the beach. He'll probably want to play with the surf. Most horses love it."

With Kim and Adam trotting behind, they rode the horses to the water's edge. Battlecry was intrigued by the rhythmic approach and retreat of the waves. He pranced along their edges, trying to give chase as the frothy water was sucked back down the sand, then crested again to rush back at him.

"He likes it!" Adam called from behind.

"He sure does." Leslie laughed. "So do I!"

Mr. D'Andrea led them along the beach at the water's edge to within a few yards of a tilted sign marking the end of public area. He unclipped the lead. "Let him canter back. I'll stay as close as I can, but I don't think you'll have any trouble."

The big horse needed no urging to stride out again. He tossed his head gleefully and gave excited little snorts as he danced in and out of the waves, growing more daring as he splashed in to his belly, then out again. Leslie breathed deeply of the salt air and sighed happily. She glanced back over her shoulder and saw the others cantering behind, having fun. When they reached the opposite boundary of the beach, she turned Battlecry and called to her father, "I'm going to let him out."

"Okay. Just keep him in hand. None of us can keep up with you."

Leslie nodded her understanding, then spoke to the horse. "Let's gallop, boy—really let her rip!" Battlecry whuffed, and with the slightest pressure of Leslie's legs he was off, pounding down the long stretch of wet sand with mane and tail flying. Leslie gripped his sides with her knees and bent low over his neck. The salty air stung her eyes and whipped her blond hair back from her cheeks. "Atta boy!" She laughed as they raced along between blue water and pale sand. At the end of the beach she checked Battlecry's speed and turned him, and they galloped off again. The stallion loved this new game. They swept past the others, who'd moved up higher on the beach. Leslie lifted her hand in a triumphant wave, then settled low in the saddle again. She let Battle run until he was ready to slow the pace on his own. When he dropped back into a canter, he was still exhilarated and barely winded. Leslie patted his arched neck as the others rode up. "So how did he look?" Leslie asked eagerly.

Adam gave her a big smile. "What do you think?"

"He felt great!" Leslie said breathlessly as she returned his smile.

"You reminded Romeo and Desert that they used to be racehorses," Adam added. "They were hot to go after him. Of course, it was no contest."

"I don't think Desert's run that fast since I've had him." Kim laughed.

They trotted the horses back along the water's edge, letting them play in the waves for a while, then Mr. D'Andrea clipped the lead to Battlecry's bridle and they headed back to the farm.

"You didn't tell me what you thought," Leslie said to her father. "Was something wrong?"

Her father smiled. "No—far from it. His action

was fine. I was just wondering if it's time to start thinking of entering him in a race."

"Do you mean it?" Leslie gasped. This was more than she'd expected.

"Don't jump the gun. I'm not saying he's ready yet. You've still got to work him from the gate, and he's got to do some really decent breezes before I'll make any decisions."

"But he's getting there?"

"He's getting there. And, frankly, I'm amazed."

Leslie glanced back over her shoulder at Kim and Adam and lifted her brows. Adam gave her a thumbs-up and Kim laughed.

6

Very early on a misty May morning, Leslie urged Battlecry toward the starting gate that had been rolled across the training oval. Mr. D'Andrea was considering entering him in a small allowance race at Rockingham, a track in New Hampshire, and this was the final test to decide if Battle was ready.

Leslie saw her father, her mother, and Nick Bates standing by the rail at the far end of the stretch. They were all looking eager and intense, waiting to see Leslie break the big horse from the gate and breeze him a mile.

Leslie felt her pulse racing, but she couldn't let Battle feel her nervous excitement or he'd never behave. Jeremy was waiting by one of the starting gate slots. He'd help load them in, close the doors, trigger the gate open, and then quickly pull it off the track before they'd finished the first lap.

Battlecry knew what the starting gate was about —he'd been in one many times before—but they all knew he'd acted up in the gate before, too. As Leslie urged him toward the open slot, she felt his muscles quivering, but she didn't think it was from fear. Jeremy took hold of the stallion's bridle to lead him in. Battlecry snorted and danced his hindquarters around.

"Easy," Leslie said soothingly, but she felt a stab of panic. What would she do if he reared in the gate like he'd done in the past? "Nice and slow," she said, rubbing Battle's neck. "Show me your good side today. I want to be proud of you."

Battle's ears flicked back as he listened. He stopped his prancing, but Jeremy frankly looked scared. "I'll get him in," Leslie said quietly. "Just close the gate behind us, and be quick with the starter button."

Jeremy nodded and released Battlecry just short of the entrance to the narrow slot.

Leslie tightened her legs slightly on the horse's sides. "Go on in. There's nothing to be afraid of." Battlecry snorted, but he walked forward. "That's it, boy." So far, so good.

Jeremy closed the gate doors behind them. Leslie readied herself, settling in the racing saddle and gripping a handful of mane with each of the reins. She didn't want to be left at the gate when Battlecry surged out! The black horse was ready and alert—Leslie wondered if he could somehow sense that this was important. She looked straight between his ears and waited.

The gate doors sprang open. "Go!" she cried, thrusting her arms forward. With a gigantic leap, Battlecry surged out onto the track, nearly pulling Leslie's arms from their sockets.

She left him alone for the first few strides, then settled the horse closer to the inside rail, keeping steady tension on the reins and reserving his speed for the last half mile. But still they were flying as they pounded down the dirt track. Battle's mane whipped back into her face as Leslie crouched over his withers. The rush of air stung her eyes.

They swept around the half-mile track. The turns were much tighter than they would be at a standard mile-or-longer racetrack, but Battle was bending smoothly around them, showing no sign of getting off balance. He was amazingly agile and precise in his movements for a horse his size.

As they rounded the turn near the end of the first half mile, Leslie knew their time was good. She'd exercised enough horses to be able to sense the passing fractions. As they roared up to the marker pole, Leslie let out some rein, clucked, and cried, "Go to it!"

Battle thrust his head forward, taking up the rein and lengthening his stride. His exhilarating speed took Leslie's breath away. Though her eyes blurred from the rushing wind and his stinging mane, she was in heaven. The sensation of roaring down the track in perfect communion with a powerful animal was pure bliss. And she knew the horse beneath her could feel it too.

Hooves pounding, they came off the far turn. Ahead were her father and Nick, stopwatches in hand. Leslie saw the pole whizzing up on her inside, and she and Battlecry thundered past. Only then did Leslie draw back on the reins and stand high in the stirrups. After their arduous weeks of training, Battle had finally learned to respond instantly to those commands. He slowed his strides and gradually dropped back into a canter, then a trot as Leslie turned him. Battlecry seemed to know that his star was shining after the performance he'd just given. At Leslie's words of praise, he tossed his head and lifted his feet like a dancer.

"Oh, Battle! That was fantastic! You're wonderful—I knew you could do it," Leslie whispered.

They were met by a cheer as they rode off the oval. "Incredible!" Nick Bates shouted. "A minute thirty-five seconds, even with those tight turns! And this horse could have been mine! I don't believe it."

Leslie's mother smiled up at her daughter. "It seems we were right about this guy."

"Don't rub it in," her husband said with a laugh. "It took some darned hard work getting him here! Nick, did I tell you that he jumped the paddock fence again last week and went over to the mares? I was ready to kill him!"

"Maybe you'll get a foal out of it," Nick Bates said, grinning.

"That's all I need. The rescue operation barely breaks even as it is. And no one's going to be impressed with his bloodlines."

"I don't know," Nick said. "If he comes along like I think he's going to, it could change a few minds."

"We haven't even run him yet. Let's not get carried away."

"We're going to Rockingham!" Leslie told Adam, Kim, and Gabby when they met at school later that morning. "Dad's decided to enter Battle in a race there next weekend."

"That little track up in New Hampshire?" Kim asked. "Why not here in New York?"

Leslie pushed some blond hair from her eyes as she reached down in the bottom of her locker. "Dad thinks it will be a good testing ground—he's still worried about how Battle will behave when he's actually at the track. I mean, the horse could do what he's done before and get crazy. Better to try him up there, without all Dad's trainer friends watching."

"He's that worried, huh? What about you?" Adam asked.

"I think Battle's going to do fine!" Leslie wished she felt as sure as her words sounded. But truthfully, she wasn't sure either how the horse would react to all the trackside excitement. His past record was dismal.

"If you were racing at Belmont, we could all go

together," Gabby said. "Are you going with Battle to New Hampshire?"

"Yup. Dad's bringing him up on Thursday. Mom and I will drive up Friday afternoon."

"But you'll miss the spring dance!" Kim cried. "I thought you two were going to come. You had your dress picked out and everything. Adam, can't you talk her out of it?"

Adam made a face. "Nah. I know, I'm being stood up for a horse. But I don't mind. This race is too important. We're going to dinner and the movies tonight instead."

"If Les doesn't fall asleep in her seat," Kim teased. "I don't know how you can stand getting up at five every morning, Leslie."

"I'm used to it." Leslie gave Adam a shining smile. She was thankful that he was so supportive of her plans for Battlecry.

On Friday afternoon, Mrs. D'Andrea picked Leslie up at school. The car was already packed with their overnight bags and a cooler filled with sandwiches and drinks. Adam walked Leslie out to the car and paused to say hello to Leslie's mother and wish them good luck.

"So I guess you like this stallion too," he said to Mrs. D'Andrea.

"I've definitely got a soft spot for him," she replied with a smile. "He's had a rough time. I know other people in the business will think we're crazy

70

to even try him again, but I really don't think he's come into his own until now."

"I'll be rooting for you. I'll call you Sunday night, Les."

"Thanks." She smiled at him and returned the warm squeeze of his hand. "If Battlecry wins, you'll probably hear me screaming all the way from New Hampshire!"

The drive north through rolling New England countryside took about five hours. In mid May, the trees wore a covering of fresh foliage, and the grass was a brilliant green. After a while, Leslie fell asleep and was only wakened by her mother's voice.

"Whew!" Mrs. D'Andrea said as she turned the car into the backside parking lot at the track. "I'm glad that's over. It'll feel good to stretch my legs. Your father said he'd wait here for us at the barn, then we can all go over to the motel. I guess you're anxious to see Battle."

"Yeah, I am." Leslie crawled out of the car, stretching her cramped muscles.

They locked the car and set off toward the line of wooden stabling barns. The cool night air was crystal clear and smelled of pine. Leslie took a deep breath.

"Some change from New York smog, isn't it?" Her mother smiled. "Let's see how good your father's directions are. Left here, I think, three barns down, then right." As they walked under the trees, they saw other backside personnel moving about, but it was peaceful in the barns with the horses fed and settled for the night. Grooms and trainers, talking quietly, were making final checks on their charges. The backside would begin to buzz at dawn, with the morning workouts.

Leslie had spent many, many hours at the big New York and New Jersey tracks with her father. Rockingham seemed countrified in comparison; the barns smaller, the paths narrower.

"There's Dad," Leslie said as they rounded the corner of a stable building. Mr. D'Andrea saw them and waved.

"You made better time than I thought," he said, giving them each a hug.

"How's Battle?" Leslie asked quickly.

"He's been better." Her dad's face gave nothing away.

"Oh no. He's acting up?" Leslie felt a hollow pit form in her stomach.

"The longer he's here, the worse he gets. Being at the track seems to be bringing out his old behavior. He bit one of the grooms who made the mistake of turning his back on him. I ended up having to walk him myself, since no one else wanted to handle him. I should have brought Jeremy up."

"What good would that have done? Jeremy won't go near him either," Leslie said.

"Well, I'm glad you're here. You can take over his grooming. Go talk to him. He's two stalls down."

The stallion had heard Leslie's voice and already had his elegant black head over the stall door. He let out a piercing whinny when he saw her.

Leslie hurried over. "So you've been acting like a brat," she said firmly as she reached the stall. Battlecry momentarily flattened his ears and nipped at her shirt, telling her that she wasn't going to be easily forgiven for deserting him.

"Cut it out," Leslie said briskly. "I know you're mad, but biting me isn't going to get you anywhere."

The horse released her shirt. Fortunately it was baggy, so his teeth hadn't connected with her skin. His ears gradually came forward, but he looked far from pacified.

Leslie lifted the lid of the tack box outside his stall and pulled a carrot from the bag always kept inside. Battlecry whuffed in expectation. "Don't expect any more of these if you don't behave," Leslie warned. He bobbed his head, quickly lipped up the carrot from her palm, and noisily crunched down on it. "I mean it," Leslie added.

Battle butted her shoulder gently with his head.

"You can be so sweet when you want to," Leslie said, chuckling, "but you don't fool me."

Her parents walked up behind her. "Better already," her father said.

"For now. Did you try him on the track this morning?" Leslie asked.

"Karen took him out. Let's just say he didn't try *too* hard to unseat her."

73

Leslie frowned. Her father had already lined up one of the better regular Rockingham jockeys, Karen Jenkins, to ride Battlecry in the following day's race. Since Leslie had had success in working with the stallion, Mr. D'Andrea thought staying with a woman jockey would be wise. "She was able to handle him?" Leslie asked.

"I'd warned her that he'd test her, so she was prepared. She's a good rider—wouldn't let him get away with anything. My main fear is that he'll decide to be stubborn tomorrow and not run at all."

They stayed at the barn until Battlecry seemed more settled and quiet, but they were back at the track by five the next morning with a long day to look forward to.

Fortunately Battlecry had spent a peaceful night, but he was definitely ready to get out of his stall when Leslie arrived. His feed had already been cut back in preparation for the race; Leslie wasn't sure if he remembered what that meant, but he was wired.

As busy as she was bathing and grooming Battlecry, the hours before the race seemed to drag for Leslie. Their race wouldn't go off until midafternoon. It was a maiden allowance race for horses three years old and up who had never won a race. Battlecry, at five, would be the oldest horse in the field, and Leslie heard plenty of talk about it after she'd settled Battlecry in his stall again and sat eating her lunch on a nearby bench.

Two regular Rockingham trainers were talking. One had a horse in the same race as Battlecry. "A five-year-old maiden? Can't figure what D'Andrea's up to. Take a look at the form. Horse hasn't raced in over a year, and when he did, he ran dead last, beat by seventeen lengths!"

"But he won't be running against as good company up here."

"I watched Karen work him yesterday. She had her hands full, and when she finally got him to settle, he breezed out a lousy quarter. That horse doesn't look like he can get out of his own way."

Leslie knew her father hadn't been trying to impress anyone with the previous day's workout; he'd only wanted Battlecry to get used to the jockey and the track. But still, the other trainers' words stung. *Well, we'll show them!* Leslie thought as she crumpled up her napkin and tossed it in the nearest trash can.

She told her parents what she'd heard, but neither of them seemed upset by it. "I'd have my doubts too," her father said, "if I was judging him on past performance. But if he runs his race well today, people will start looking at him a little differently."

When post time finally arrived, Leslie saw from the odds board that the bettors didn't have any confidence in Battlecry either—he was going off at 80 to 1! The odds would have been even higher, but one three-year-old in the field had never raced at all. Battlecry at least had been on a racetrack. But the big horse hadn't impressed anyone with his behavior in the walking ring. Physically, he was beautiful—tall, elegant, with his coal black coat shimmering and his long mane and tail flowing like silk. But it had been all Leslie could do to control him as he skittered around and jerked at the lead shank. He'd worked up a nervous sweat before his petite, dark-haired jockey even mounted. She hadn't looked too happy as she'd settled in the saddle, but she hadn't let Battlecry get the better of her. After listening carefully to Mr. D'Andrea's instructions, she nodded, then said quietly but firmly to the horse, "We're going out there and you're going to run a good race!"

But as Leslie looked down from their grandstand seats and watched the field go into the starting gate, she felt a lump rise in her throat. Battlecry wasn't finished with his high jinks yet. It took the efforts of three assistants to load the muscular black animal into the gate—one at his head, two pushing from behind. If only Leslie could go down and be with him!

"Behave yourself, you jerk," she whispered under her breath. But once inside, Battlecry stood calmly with his ears pricked forward. He obviously knew what was coming, but would he run like he did when Leslie was riding him?

The gate doors flipped open to ringing bells. The race was on! Battlecry was in post position five in the eight-horse field. Leslie sighed with relief to see him get off cleanly, surging right up with the leaders. Her father had told Karen to try to pace him if she could for the first three quarters of a mile, but that Battlecry would probably want to run in the lead. The jockey had looked skeptical, probably thinking of all Battlecry's last-place finishes and figuring the horse would burn himself out long before the race was over.

Karen was following instructions, though. Battlecry pulled her straight to the lead, but she kept a firm hold as she eased him in along the rail. Concorde Jimmy, another speed horse, was in the race, and he wasn't going to let Battlecry have the lead unchallenged. Leslie held her breath as he raced up alongside Battlecry, but the black horse increased his speed to match.

"Karen's having trouble holding him," Mr. D'Andrea muttered next to Leslie. "Looks like we're going to have a speed duel."

He was right. Leslie sat forward on her seat when she heard the track announcer cry out the fractions for the first quarter and a half. "Twenty-one and three! Forty-four! Battlecry, one of the longest shots on the board, holding on to a short lead. Concorde Jimmy's pressing him . . . six lengths back to Waddley . . . then High Intent . . . Stone Mountain hasn't made his move yet . . ."

The two horses pounded down the backstretch, leaving the rest of the field far behind. "Hold on, Battle!" Leslie groaned. They swept into the far turn, hooves pounding, manes flying. Karen was curled low over Battle's withers. Even at this distance, Leslie could see Battle's powerful muscles bunching and stretching as he continued his relentless pace.

"Concorde Jimmy's dropping back!" the announcer called. "The speed's too much for him, but Karen Jenkins still has some horse left. Battlecry's drawing off without being asked . . . under a hand ride! Five, now six lengths! Stone Mountain's making his move on the outside . . . but Battlecry is walking away from this field! Jenkins still hasn't lifted her whip! And they're under the wire! Battlecry a decisive winner today, setting a new track record! Ten lengths back to Stone Mountain . . . Concorde Jimmy hangs in for third . . ."

"He did it!" the D'Andreas screamed as Battlecry went under the wire. Leslie jumped up and down, then turned and hugged both her parents. Her father was laughing. "What a race! He chewed them up and spit them out!" Leslie watched proudly as Battlecry pranced arrogantly off the track, his muscles rippling under his gleaming black coat. "Come on. You guys and Nick were right," her father added. "Let's get down to the winner's circle!"

Leslie and her parents scrambled past people as they made their way to the exit. Leslie's head was spinning, and her breath was as short as if she had been riding Battle herself. They made their way to the winner's circle, past the bustling crowd of spectators standing near the rail.

But Leslie wasn't paying any attention to them.

She only had eyes for Battlecry, who had just shown so decisively that her faith in him was justified.

"Battle, Battle," Leslie whispered, throwing her arms around his neck for the first time. The big horse didn't seem surprised, but reacted with unexpected gentleness as he softly whoofed into Leslie's blond hair. "I knew you could do it, boy. I knew you could." Battlecry nudged Leslie gently, his ears flicked forward to catch her words.

Leslie turned and smiled up at Karen. "So how was it?"

"Incredible," Karen gasped. "I sure wasn't expecting a ride like that when I got on his back! He's unbelievable. Speed and stamina. Where'd you find this guy? Where's he been for five years?" She swung off the horse and stood next to Leslie.

"Growing up," Mrs. D'Andrea told her. "And he nearly got made into stallion steak in the process."

"You're kidding!"

"We got him off the auction block after outbidding the butcher."

"Good grief!" Karen cried. "What a waste that would have been!"

A gray-haired man in a sports jacket pushed up to the D'Andreas. "Did I hear you right?" he asked with a frown. "Did this horse almost go to the meat packer?"

"That's right."

"What a story! Give me the details—oh, I'm Tony Mazzi, rep for *The Racing Times* up here."

Tony Mazzi wasn't the only one listening as the D'Andreas told Battlecry's story. Leslie saw others leaning forward eagerly as she threw a sheet over Battlecry. "Well, boy," she murmured to the stallion. "This is just the beginning. Get used to it."

Much later, after Leslie had cooled Battlecry off, washed him, and curried him till he shone, she asked her father what he planned for the future.

"Let's face it," he answered, leaning against the stable wall. "He didn't beat the best horses in the world today, but considering the way he did it, I think we should go to Belmont and put him in some decent allowance company."

"All right!" Leslie cried.

"There's more good news," her mother said. "That five dollars you gave me to bet earned you about four hundred dollars. With the winner's purse and the little your father and I bet, it looks like Battlecry's just paid for a full year's board and entry fees in one fell swoop. And there's some left over." She gave her daughter a hug and a kiss.

"The extra money could save a couple more horses," Leslie said. "What do you think, Battle?"

The horse interrupted his meal long enough to thrust his head over the stall door and whinny.

7

"This traffic is awful!" Kim groaned as she inched her jeep along in the bumper-to-bumper congestion on the Long Island Expressway. It was hot for a late May morning, and they had the jeep windows wide open.

"We've got plenty of time before the race," Gabby said from the front passenger seat.

"But Les wants to spend some time with Battlecry beforehand. Right?" Kim asked Leslie and Adam, who were sitting in the backseat.

"We've only got one more exit to go," Leslie said. "The traffic won't be so bad after that."

"I hope. I want to have some time to see the backside, like you promised."

"You won't get to see all of it. It's huge," Leslie answered. "But there'll be plenty of time before the first race. Dad's got a permanent groom at Belmont, so after I say hello to Battlecry, I can give you guys a tour. I just hope he's not acting up like he did at Rockingham."

"He's already been there for three days," Adam said.

"Mmm, but he knows when he's racing, and that could be enough to set him off."

"At least he'll have the same jockey as for his last race."

"Karen jumped at the chance to come down to ride him," Leslie said. "She's ridden at Belmont before, but only when a Rockingham shipper brings down a horse. It's a hard place to break into."

Kim reached their exit and gunned the jeep down the ramp. "Okay, give me directions from here," she told Leslie.

Leslie did, and a short time later they pulled into one of the backside parking lots. After Kim left the jeep beneath a shady tree, the four of them set off toward Mr. D'Andrea's stabling area. A half dozen of the horses he trained had regular stabling on the track, and Leslie expertly wove her way in that direction. With the traffic, the trip had taken twice as long as they'd expected, and it was close to eleven. Battlecry was running in an allowance race at one o'clock—the first race on the card—so they really didn't have much time.

Leslie's parents and Karen Jenkins were standing outside Battlecry's stall as Leslie and the others walked up.

"We thought you'd never get here!" Mrs. D'Andrea cried. "Traffic?"

"Yeah, and we got a late start because Kim had to drop her brother off at the Y. How's Battle?"

"Surprisingly calm, but let's keep our fingers crossed."

Leslie smiled at Karen and quickly introduced her friends, then went to Battlecry, who had his handsome black head over the stall door and was bobbing it up and down. "Yes, I'm coming to talk to you," she said. "I hear you've been good." He eyed her meaningfully. "Sorry, no carrots, boy. It's too close to race time. But if you win this one, I'll give you a bagful."

Battlecry stomped and reached out to lip Leslie's shirt gently. "Come on, you're not that hungry," Leslie said. "And you don't have long to wait." She turned to Karen. "How'd he do when you worked him?"

"Good. Maybe he's just getting used to me, but he didn't try to pitch me, and he breezed out a nice half mile."

"That's what Dad said."

"We got some interested looks when we rode off," the jockey added. "A couple of people remember him from before. I think they were waiting for him to explode."

"And not in a forward direction," Mr. D'Andrea said, laughing. "The other trainers still think I'm crazy to even think of running him."

"But what about the race at Rockingham?" Adam asked.

"Small track, lousy field. They weren't impressed. But looking at the horses we're up against today, I think we've got a good chance of winning —if he behaves himself in the gate, gets off clean, doesn't get blocked or bumped, and runs the race he did last time."

Leslie grinned and nodded. Her father was sounding more like himself—very cautious. "Do you need me to help with anything now?"

"No, he's set. Go give your friends a tour. Just be sure you're back before we go to the saddling paddock."

"Oh, I will!"

For the next hour Leslie, Kim, Gabby, and Adam covered as much of the backside as they could. Leslie waved to people she knew and pointed out the stalls of several of the best horses in the country. Most of them were at the track being readied for the Belmont Stakes, the third leg of the Triple Crown for three-year-olds, and for the Nassau County Handicap, part of the American Championship Racing Series for older horses.

"So that's Zinger!" Kim gazed at a sleek chestnut colt who had his head over his stall door. His groom was positioned outside, keeping people away. She nudged Gabby. "He won the Triple Crown last year!"

"I may not be as nutty about horses as you and

Les," Gabby complained, "but even I know that much."

"He's been running in the American Championship series this year," Leslie told them. "There are seven races in it, all over the country, and he's won two so far."

"Hey, that's where you can head Battlecry!" Gabby exclaimed.

"Are you kidding?" Leslie laughed. "We're not in the same league!"

"You might be, though."

"That would be pretty miraculous. Battle's won one race. The horses in those fields have won dozens of Grade 1's." Leslie checked her watch. "I've got to get back. Why don't you all head to the grandstand? I'll be leading Battle in the walking ring, but you guys can watch."

Adam leaned close to Leslie's ear as they walked back. "Thanks for inviting me. This is fantastic. I'm glad I came."

"Me too," she told him, and squeezed his hand.

"He's winning! He's winning!" Leslie screamed as Battlecry surged down the Belmont stretch toward the wire. She was jumping up and down and hugging her parents, Adam, Kim, and Gabby all at once. "He's doing it again! He's done it!" Battlecry's powerful form swept under the wire, eight lengths ahead of the next horse in the field. "He set another track record! Oh, my God!"

Adam put his arm around Leslie's shoulders

and squeezed them tight. "Wow, can that horse run! He was booking!"

"Battlecry, a five-year-old who only won his maiden two weeks ago!" the announcer called. "I think we'll be seeing more of this newcomer from Phil D'Andrea's stable."

Kim and Gabby were almost as excited as Leslie. "Congratulations! It's absolutely amazing watching him run," Kim said. "Even if I still wouldn't get on his back myself. You've got to run him in the Nassau County Handicap . . . in the American Championship series, Mr. D'Andrea!"

Leslie's father laughed. "You're jumping the gun a little, don't you think? Two allowance wins don't exactly make him champion caliber."

"Yeah, but you won't know if he could be a champion unless you try," Gabby said with a grin.

"You guys are getting carried away. But we've got a horse in the winner's circle. Come on." Mr. D'Andrea was smiling as they all trooped down the grandstand steps.

When they reached the winner's circle, Leslie ran up and hugged Battlecry—hard. In the past two weeks, he had gotten much less skittish about Leslie's showing him affection, and now he seemed actually to respond. He whoofed against her hair and gently snuffled into her shirt. It was as though he was saying "Thanks—thanks for believing in me."

Later, after the winner's photo was taken, congratulations made, and Leslie was leading Battlecry back to his stall, Mr. D'Andrea got more comments on the backside from reporters and fellow trainers.

"Hey, Phil," one cried, "you know how to keep secrets, don't you?"

"I told you he could surprise you," Mr. D'Andrea called back. "You guys didn't want to believe it."

"Where'd you get him? I know you didn't claim him from Hawkins. A private deal?"

"Thought you knew the story. We bought him with a bunch of retired claimers that were going to the meat farm in Jersey."

"Yeah, now I remember. I heard someone talking about a sob-story horse. This is the same one?"

"The same. He just happened to be a dozen notches better than the average we get."

"How the heck did a horse of this quality get thrown in with that bunch?"

"Have you seen his early race record?" Mr. D'Andrea kidded.

"I have," a reporter called. "Dismal. What are your plans now?"

"We'll have to think about it. I'll talk to you later, guys. I've got a horse to see to."

While all the questions were being fired at her father, Leslie kept looking up at Battlecry and smiling proudly. She couldn't help herself. "He's come out of the race looking good," she said to Mr. D'Andrea when they stopped outside Battlecry's stall.

"Amazingly good. I'll check him over more carefully when he's cooled out, and we'll have to see how he eats. But the race doesn't seem to have taken much out of him at all. Looks like it was my lucky day when you came to the farm, monster."

Battlecry arched his neck and nickered in acknowledgment. It looked as if this second win had gone right to his head.

Leslie caught her mother's eye, and they both smiled.

"Darn," Kim said, looking at her watch. "We have to get back. Actually," she said, blushing, "I have a date tonight."

"Oh yeah? Who with?" Adam teased when he saw her flushed cheeks.

"Somebody I met at the beach," Kim said mysteriously. "No one you know." She obviously didn't want to say more and quickly turned away, on the pretense of studying the horses being led past.

Her friends all lifted their brows and exchanged looks. Gabby shrugged and shook her head.

"I have to get back too," Adam said. "I have to work later this afternoon. Though I'd much rather stay here," he added with a smile to Leslie.

"You didn't forget the three of us are going to play miniature golf tonight?" Gabby asked.

"Nope," Leslie told her. "I'll be home before dinner."

"I'll give you a call when I get off work," Adam said. "And thanks a lot for inviting me."

"Yeah, thanks, Mr. and Mrs. D'Andrea. Thanks, Les," Kim and Gabby echoed.

When they were gone, Leslie walked, bathed, and fed Battlecry. She enjoyed these quiet times together, when it was just her and Battlecry. Of course, she liked it when he won races, too! She was just rubbing Battlecry's coat until it shone when Nick Bates showed up at the stall.

"He doesn't look any the worse for the wear," Nick said as he looked inside the stall at Battlecry. "He's even better than I thought."

Mr. D'Andrea walked up in time to hear Nick. He leaned against the stable wall and shrugged noncommittally.

"Hey, you don't have to put on that cautious act with me," Nick said, grinning. "I know what you've got here—these two wins weren't just good luck. No matter what they say, you've got some trainers sweating."

"We've both been around long enough to know that could change," Mr. D'Andrea said. "This guy could turn right around again—the wrong way."

"Not now, when he's had a taste of winning." Nick fingered his chin. "I think you ought to consider the Nassau County Handicap."

"You do?" Leslie gulped. She hadn't taken the suggestion seriously from Kim, but when Nick made the same suggestion, it was different. She stopped what she was doing and came to stand at the stall door.

"Nick's getting carried away with himself," her father said.

"No, I'm not. And I'm not the only one thinking that way, either. Look at his speed figures—look at the way he came out of the race. You know he can go the distance."

Mr. D'Andrea shook his head. "The Nassau's only two weeks away."

"You've got plenty of time. If he'd been racing a heavy schedule or came out of the race beat, I'd say two weeks was too soon. But that's not the case."

"Dad, won't you think about it?" Leslie put in.

"You'll have a weight advantage, too," Nick added. "With only two allowance races under his belt, he'll be assigned less weight. A horse like Zinger will probably have a dozen pounds on you."

Leslie hadn't even thought of that, but the Nassau was a handicap, where horses were assigned to carry extra weight according to their previous accomplishments. Eyeing her father closely, she could see Nick was wearing him down. Her father scowled at her, and she wiped the grin from her lips.

"Look at another side of it," Nick continued. "Think of the publicity you'll get for the rescue operation. One of your rescue horses going on to the big time. I can see the headlines—"

"Cut it out, Nick! I'll see how he does in the next few days back at the farm."

Nick knew when to quit, but when Mr. D'Andrea turned to look in the stall at his charge, Nick gave Leslie a wink.

Just because Battle had won two races didn't mean Leslie could ease up on his training schedule. She was out at the crack of dawn every morning, knowing she had a lot of horse to deal with. Battlecry was full of himself these days. He knew he'd done well—how could he help it after all the attention he'd received? Every inch of his high spiritedness was coming out: he was bucking playfully onto the track, trying to take the bit and run off with her. "Will you calm down!" she told him hotly. "You haven't exactly won Horse of the Year honors. Though," she conceded, patting his neck, "you've done pretty well for a horse nobody thought could run. But if Dad enters you in the Nassau, you're going to have to do even better!"

Battle flattened his ears, not liking the tone of her voice.

"I'm not kidding," she warned him. "We've still got a lot of work to do if you're going to run with the top horses in the country!"

"Two more weeks and we're out of here!" Adam said to Leslie when they met in the hall after chemistry one afternoon at the beginning of June.

"I can't wait," Leslie agreed. Chemistry was definitely not Leslie's favorite subject, though she knew a knowledge of chemistry came in handy in horse care.

"I don't think I did very well on that quiz." She frowned. "And tonight's more homework!"

"I'll give you a hand if you want," Adam offered. "I'm not working tonight."

"That would be great. And I suppose you want me to read through your English paper."

He grinned. "You know me too well."

"Oh, okay. It's a deal." Leslie laughed.

"Your father still hasn't decided about the Nassau?" Adam asked as they headed toward the lunchroom.

"He won't say one way or the other. It'll be a big step for Battle. Sometimes I wonder myself if he's ready. Though from the way he's acting, you'd never know he just put in a big race. My father's thinking about entry and jockey fees, too. Since we own Battle, my parents will have to come up with the money."

"What about talking to the people who give contributions to your farm?"

Leslie gave him a surprised look. "You've really been thinking about this, haven't you?"

Adam grinned sheepishly. "You've got me hooked. I want to see Battle do good."

"Thanks," Leslie said, smiling. "My mom's already talked to some of the bigger contributors, asking if they'd be interested in being sponsors, but they don't sound that interested yet. Battlecry's got to do more to prove himself before they'll put up any money. And it's not like the Nassau's his only chance. Dad will keep running him—but in smaller races."

"Well, don't give up."

"Oh, I haven't! And I have a funny feeling Nick Bates might help out."

Leslie was right about that. Neither her father nor Nick admitted that Nick had put up some of the entrance money for the Nassau, but on Sunday night, Mr. D'Andrea announced to Leslie and her mother that Battlecry was entered in the coming Saturday's race. "I'll bring him back to Belmont tomorrow so he can get a couple of works on the track," Mr. D'Andrea said. "I know you still have another week of school, Les, but maybe you could come up with me before school a couple of times. He behaves and trains better when you ride him—"

"I'll get up at three in the morning, if it means he'll run in the Nassau!" Leslie cried.

"But you have finals coming up, and I don't want your grades to slide," Mr. D'Andrea warned.

"They won't, Dad! I've got a B-plus average, and Adam and I have already started studying."

"I can drive you up and back," Mrs. D'Andrea offered.

Leslie noticed her father didn't look too certain about his decision. "Dad," she said, "I know he's never been tried against the top horses, but even if he doesn't win, it'll be good experience for him. And good publicity for us."

"Not if we end up looking like complete fools." Her father pushed back his chair and rose from the dinner table. "I'm going to check the horses. Get his tack box sorted out for the morning trip."

Leslie nodded, but when her father left the room, she turned to her mother. "Do you think he's really that worried?" she asked.

"I suppose he feels his reputation's on the line. No trainer wants to look like he's running horses way over their heads. You look better winning an allowance race than finishing at the back of the pack in a graded stakes race."

"I don't think Battlecry will finish at the back of the pack. He's better than that, and he wants to win now."

"I think so too, but he's never run against horses like these. And your father has to keep in mind that Battle is a temperamental animal. He's blown races in the past because of it, and he could do it again."

Leslie knew that was true. Her mother's words stayed in her mind as she went out to the barn. Maybe she *was* getting her hopes up a little high. It was more likely that Battle would lose the Nassau, if Leslie wanted to face facts. True, he'd set two track records—a very impressive start—but he had no experience in big, graded races. She really was being overly confident in thinking he would walk all over the field in the Nassau. He wouldn't.

As Leslie sorted through Battlecry's box, making sure there were plenty of clean bandages and towels and that everything else was in order, he stuck his head over the stall door and watched.

"You've got a big race coming up, boy," she said, reaching to pat his silky nose. He started to make a playful grab for her fingers, then seemed to think better of it. "It's going to be the biggest challenge you've had so far."

Battlecry scratched his head on the door frame and eyed her. Leslie was sure she could see intelligence in his glance.

"You don't look very impressed, but you ought to be. You may not win this one."

He snorted indignantly, as if to say, "No way!"

"I hope you're right," Leslie said. "I hope that all of us are right. I don't want my dad to look like a fool. But I'll be satisfied if you just run a good race—whether you win or lose." Closing the tack box, she rose and went into the stall to check the water and hay net. Then she reached up to give the stallion a hug around the neck. He was in a willful mood, though, and deliberately side-stepped her to prance around the stall.

"Have it your way, then," Leslie said over her shoulder. "No good-night hugs for you."

As she unlatched the stall door, she listened for a rustle in the straw behind her and wasn't the least surprised when she felt Battlecry give her a firm nudge between her shoulder blades. "Good night," she said, laughing. "See you in the morning."

Battlecry whickered. Leslie fastened the door

shut and turned to see Jeremy standing in the aisle, shaking his head.

"You're nuts the way you turn your back on him," Jeremy growled. "He could just as easily have reared up on you!"

"He's not as bad as you think, Jeremy. You just have an attitude about him, and he knows it."

"It's not only me. There aren't too many grooms on the Belmont backside who want to get near him."

"They've been listening to you talk. Anyway, you won't have to worry about him for a while. He's going to the track in the morning. We're running him in the Nassau."

"So I heard." From his tone, it sounded like Jeremy thought her parents were asking for trouble.

But Edwin walked up at that moment. "That's a good piece of news," the old man said.

8

Leslie and her mother arrived at Battlecry's Belmont stall at six on Wednesday morning to find both Mr. D'Andrea and a groom trying to hold the rearing horse.

"Oh no," Leslie groaned. It had rained heavily for two days, and except for a walk around the yard, Battlecry hadn't been out of his stall. Now he was showing his full frustration, and Leslie's father and the groom weren't the only ones witnessing the stallion's rowdiness. Several trainers, some track regulars, and a reporter Leslie recognized were standing nearby. Her father and the groom, with lead shanks clipped to each side of Battlecry's halter, managed to lever the stallion down, but within a few strides he reared again and squealed in outrage as his front hooves cleaved the air in front of him.

Leslie knew better than to approach until the

horse was down on all fours again, but she was dying to comfort him. Finally, the men held their lead shanks with both hands and managed to get Battlecry down, but he was fighting them every inch of the way. Leslie heard her father mutter under his breath, "Behave, you dumb terror!"

"Terror is right," one of the watchers said. "You expect to keep a rider on his back? Unpredictable animal."

"He didn't work out yesterday," Leslie informed the speaker.

"What do you have to do—work him a couple of miles every day just to keep him in line? And he's going to be in shape for the Nassau?"

Leslie ignored the comment and slowly approached Battlecry. Now that his feet were on the ground, at least for a moment, he could see her. "Easy, boy," she said quietly. "We're going to go out for a ride now. You can get rid of all those high spirits. Won't you like that?"

Battlecry flicked his ears toward her, but he snorted uneasily, and the whites of his eyes were showing.

"Come on, now," Leslie soothed. "You know how to behave when you want to. One whole day in your stall isn't that bad."

The horse made unhappy grunting noises, but he kept watching her and listening to her familiar voice. Leslie was close enough now to take the lead shank from the groom. She gripped it with her left hand and gently put her right hand on

Battlecry's nose. "That's it, boy. Good boy." She saw her father nod to the groom, telling him to go collect Battle's tack. Leslie was already dressed for the workout in jeans, riding boots, and helmet.

"Start walking him to the track," her father said quietly. "We'll tack him up there and get him right out."

From the tension Battlecry was putting on the lead shanks, Leslie knew he could explode again at any moment. Others seemed to notice too. Swift, uncertain looks were cast their way from backside staff leading horses to the track for morning workouts. Behind her Leslie heard someone say, "Kid's got guts if she's going to ride him."

When they finally reached the gap to the track, the groom approached quickly with saddle and bridle. Mrs. D'Andrea came up beside her husband and helped hold Battlecry as Mr. D'Andrea tacked him up.

"Be especially careful out there," her mother whispered to Leslie.

"I will, Mom." Leslie knew her mother trusted Leslie's riding skill, but in Battlecry's present state, there was always danger.

The groom and Mrs. D'Andrea held Battlecry's head as Mr. D'Andrea gave Leslie a leg into the saddle, but Battlecry knew what was coming now. The prospect of a gallop distracted him, and his ears were pricked toward the track. Leslie settled in the saddle and gathered the reins.

"Be your own judge," her father said to her.

"He's going to want a good gallop, but try to keep him in hand and reserve him until the last half mile."

Leslie understood exactly what her father wanted. She just hoped she could keep the big horse in hand for the first half mile. If not, she'd have to start breezing him earlier and hope he'd pull up at a mile.

She started Battlecry forward. A small crowd had gathered at the gap, and Leslie knew they were paying special attention to her and Battlecry. In his excitement Battlecry lunged against the bit and half reared, then tried to break straight into a canter. The big horse was definitely giving the spectators a clear showing of his worst side. Leslie prayed he would settle down before he unseated her. Her hands were tight on the reins, her weight was back in the saddle, and with the longer stirrups of the exercise saddle, she could use her legs to cement herself to the horse. "Don't try any funny stuff," she told him quietly. "You'll get your chance to run." At the same time she firmly but gently pressed her legs against his sides, communicating to him that she wanted him to settle down in a trot.

Battlecry responded with an arched-neck trot up the oval. His legs were working like pistons, telling Leslie that he was obeying her only under duress. When she let him out into a canter, he finally started to settle in a little. Still, Leslie had every nerve ending alert. They continued to move at a canter down the center of the track, well away from any other horses, into the far turn. Leslie looked ahead to the wire, where she would start his gallop. They were an eighth of a mile short of the wire when Battlecry decided he'd had enough of the slow pace. Other horses were ahead of him, doing their own workouts. Battlecry began throwing up his head and fighting for more rein. Leslie's hands and arms started to ache from the effort of holding him. With jerky, uneven strides, Battlecry fought his way forward until Leslie finally gave him an extra inch of rein.

Suddenly he was off, breaking into a full gallop —but at much too fast a pace. The hold Leslie had on his reins didn't seem to faze him at all, and he ignored her. "You creep, Battle!" she muttered through gritted teeth. "Don't go this fast so soon!" But her voice was blown away in the wind sweeping past them. Leslie was sure Battle was laughing at her as they thundered around the clubhouse turn, down the backstretch. All she could do now was stay on him and see how much horse she had left at the half-mile pole, when she was supposed to breeze him. *Supposed* to—they were *already* breezing!

They came off the backstretch and into the far turn. Battle showed no signs of losing momentum. In fact, he was still fighting for more rein. At the half-mile pole, Leslie knew he was still going strong, but he would be racing in three days. It would be a disaster to let Battlecry use himself up in a workout! She couldn't let him out any more. She'd have to hold him.

Battlecry was furious. With a forward thrust of his head, he tried to force the reins between Leslie's burning fingers. Her hands felt raw, but she wouldn't give him more rein. They came down the last half mile of track battling wills all the way.

In the end Leslie won, but as she finally pulled the angry horse down into a canter, she began to wonder if she'd done the right thing. Battlecry's neck was lathered in sweat, and she knew it wasn't caused only by his exertions.

"I'm sorry, Battle, but I just couldn't let you run all the way out today. Not when you've got a big a race on Saturday."

Battlecry shook his head angrily and chomped on the bit as if he wanted to break it in two. He sidestepped a little as Leslie aimed him toward the track gap.

Leslie sighed as she rode off the track. A lot of staring faces were aimed her way, and she was almost afraid to look at her father's expression.

Mr. D'Andrea didn't say a word as he took Battlecry's head and clipped a lead to the bridle of the overexcited horse.

"I know," Leslie burst out. "I shouldn't have held him . . . but I kept thinking of the race on Saturday. I didn't want him to burn himself out. But he's mad as all get out . . ."

Her father looked up. He wasn't angry—more frustrated than anything. "You did the only thing you could," he said. "If you'd let him run, it could have blown any chance we have in the Nassau. Then again, we don't know the limits of this guy's stamina yet. He might have been able to work a fast mile and a half today and still have come back strong. But it's too big a chance to take. We'll just have to hope this workout didn't frustrate him so much that he won't run when we want him to."

"Did you bother to clock him?" Leslie asked as she dismounted.

"I did. Very nice, but his behavior is what's raising comments—not exactly flattering ones, either."

The Friday afternoon before the Nassau, all the kids from Leslie's high school were having a beach party at The Neck, a popular spot about thirty minutes from Leslie's house. Even though Battle's big race was the next day, Leslie didn't want to miss the party.

"Go and have a good time," her mother told her when they got back from Belmont that morning. "It's better if Battle takes it easy in his stall this afternoon anyway. Adam's picking you up?"

"Yes, his mother lent him her car for the afternoon."

"Have fun. You deserve it after the work you've put in. Especially after getting an A on your English final."

"But I'll be lucky if I got a C in chemistry," Leslie said with a wry smile.

The beach was already packed by the time

Adam and Leslie arrived after school. High-school kids from every class had taken over the whole end of the sweeping arc of sand. A volleyball game was already in progress, and Frisbees were flying through the air. Some people were out in the water or lying around in the sun, starting their summer tans.

Leslie and Adam spotted some of their friends and spread out their own blanket nearby. Gabby ran over. "Great party!" she gasped. "Want to get in the volleyball game? We need two more players."

"Sure." Leslie and Adam jumped up. The game was intense but fun, and forty-five minutes later they were all hot, thirsty, and laughing. Gabby followed them back to the blanket and flopped down on it. Adam reached in the cooler and got out three cold drinks.

"Where's Kim?" Leslie asked, suddenly realizing she hadn't seen her all afternoon. She knew Kim and Gabby had driven over together.

Gabby scowled. "Way down at the end. She disappeared almost as soon as we got here."

"Really?" Leslie squinted down the beach. She saw Kim's shining black hair and slim figure in a bright pink bikini. But she was with some people Leslie didn't recognize. They looked older, like college kids. "Who's she with?"

"I don't know all of them, but see that blond guy standing next to her? That's Jared Rawson. He graduated last year. I've seen him around town; he rides a big Yamaha. I'm not sure if he's in college or what, but I think that's who she went out with the Saturday we went to the races with you. I'm pretty sure she's seen him since, too."

Leslie had been so busy getting Battle ready for the Nassau that she hadn't seen much of Kim the past two weeks, except at school. Kim hadn't said anything at all about a new boyfriend. "She hasn't told you about him?" Leslie asked Gabby.

"Nope. I've just noticed she's acting funny, like she's got a big secret."

Adam had been listening. "I know him," he said. "He's bad news. He's dropped out of college and has his own apartment. I've heard he's had some wild parties that the cops had to break up."

"You're kidding!" Leslie gasped. "That doesn't sound like Kim at all."

"Well, he's awful cute," Gabby said.

"Kim's no dummy," Adam said. "She'll figure it out for herself."

Leslie frowned thoughtfully, then started when someone called out to her, "Leslie! Catch!" She jumped up from the blanket and neatly caught the Frisbee that was flying toward her. She cast it back with one smooth swing of her arm.

"Nice! Come on and play, you guys."

The three of them got up and jogged toward the Frisbee players.

When Adam dropped Leslie off at the farm at nine that night, she felt sunburned and pleasantly tired. He leaned over and gave her a kiss. "That was fun."

"I had an absolutely great time," she said with a sleepy smile.

"I wish I could come to the race tomorrow, but I really can't get a day off from work. I tried."

"That's okay. Besides, you need the money if you're going to buy that car." Adam's neighbor was selling a dented but mechanically sound eight-year-old Mustang, and Adam needed transportation other than his moped.

"I'll be thinking about you, though," he said. "I may be able to watch the race on the TV in the bar, but I'll call you as soon as I get home."

"I hope I'll have good news." They kissed again before Leslie went inside. When she reached her bedroom, after talking for a few minutes to her parents, she quickly changed into her nightgown, went to the bathroom to brush her teeth, then climbed blissfully in bed. It had been a wonderful afternoon, but she was totally exhausted—and tomorrow would be a very busy day.

9

Both the Nassau County Handicap and the Belmont Stakes were being run that Saturday afternoon, and the track was mobbed. Leslie stood near the saddling paddock and watched as a well-known television sports commentator faced his cameras to give a preview of the Nassau. Behind her, her father had Battlecry in one of the saddling stalls, hoping that would help to keep the big horse quiet until race time. For the moment, Battle was behaving like a perfect gentleman. Leslie had her doubts about how long that would last. Being at the track definitely brought out the worst in him.

Since Wednesday's workout, he'd been moody and unpredictable. He'd barely lifted a hoof during their Thursday work—his last before the race —but then he'd gone back to the barn and tried to kick down his stall. They'd finally put him in crossties and closed the stall door. The last two mornings, Leslie had taken him for long walks, and he hadn't made either one very pleasurable. Leslie frankly didn't know what to expect in the race ahead.

She listened as the commentator spoke into his hand-held microphone. "We've given you a quick look at the stars in the field for the Nassau County Handicap: Zinger, last year's Triple Crown winner and one of the top older horses in the country this year, with wins in the Santa Anita and Oaklawn handicaps under his belt, and Wishful, winner of the Pimlico Special and runner-up in the Donn. But there's another horse who's been garnering some attention—the longest shot on the board . . ."

Leslie saw the camera suddenly swing to focus on Battlecry.

". . . a big, seventeen-hand five-year-old called Battlecry. This unknown has jumped into the racing picture in the last month with two back-to-back allowance wins—setting two track records. But his history is far more intriguing. In eight starts as a three- and four-year-old here at Belmont, he failed miserably, gained a reputation for being a terror on backside and track, and was a hoofbeat away from being shipped to the butcher. Then in stepped New York trainer Phil D'Andrea of D'Andrea Farm on Long Island to rescue this black horse off the auction block—for only four hundred and fifty dollars!" The commentator smiled. "D'Andrea seems to have had some insight the rest of us don't share.

"Battlecry could certainly win any beauty contests here today—as viewers can see, he's a magnificent-looking animal. He had a bullet workout here earlier this week, but he's never run in stakes company before. Is he in over his head with this field today? That remains to be seen. At 50 to 1 odds, he's certainly worth a two-dollar bet!"

"At least he's consistent as a very long shot," Leslie's mother said in her ear.

Leslie smiled, but bit her lip. "I don't know, Mom. I'm kind of worried about this race. He's acting too quiet."

As if on cue, a piercing whinny sounded behind them. They swung around to see Battlecry rearing as Mr. D'Andrea led him out of the box. "Here we go!" Leslie said as she rushed over to help. Battlecry's halo had definitely slipped.

Everyone was staring as Leslie hurried around to the other side of Battle's head and took a firm hold on his bridle. "Easy, now," she soothed. "It's just another race, and you've got their attention."

"At least he waited until I got him saddled," Mr. D'Andrea said tersely as they fought to hold Battlecry's head. "I don't know what gets into this guy."

"He knew it was almost race time. Easy, boy, calm down."

Mr. D'Andrea grunted. "We've still got to get him around the walking ring. I'll go with you, but this is probably better than the sleeping giant we had a few minutes ago."

"He's acting the same as he did before his last two races—and he won. Come on, Battle," she added to the horse, "just calm down a little."

As they moved forward around the walking ring, Battlecry stopped trying to rear, but he skittered, jerked his head around, nipped at Leslie's shoulder, called out challenges to the other horses in the walking ring, and generally showed off his worst behavior for all the spectators. And they certainly were watching his performance with awed and slightly nervous expressions.

"Guess they thought his reputation was exaggerated," Leslie whispered to her father.

Mr. D'Andrea gave a short, dry laugh.

When finally it was time for the jockeys to mount, Leslie saw Karen approach. Surprisingly, she didn't look upset at the thought of mounting the fireball in front of her. But Battlecry hadn't finished with his act yet. He shied as Karen tried to get a leg up, then laid back his ears and raked the ground with a front hoof.

"You're not scaring me," Karen said to him in a mild voice. "We've been here before, remember."

"She's got your number, Battle," Leslie said with a chuckle.

Battlecry snorted, but his ears came up, and he stood still just long enough for Mr. D'Andrea to give Karen a quick leg into the saddle.

"I don't have to tell you the competition's different," Mr. D'Andrea said to the jockey as they all circled the walking ring once more. "I doubt that you'll be able to pace him much, but if you can reserve him just off the leaders, try. That'll surprise some of the jocks because they're looking at him to be one of the pacesetting speed horses. Zinger runs just off the pace. Wishful likes to close. Watch for both of them coming at you at the quarter pole. I know I'm sounding pretty confident for a 50 to 1 shot, but I honestly believe that if he decides to run his race, he'll be at or near the lead and will give them a run for their money."

"I believe it too," Karen said firmly. "He's going to surprise a lot of people."

"Let's hope. Okay, get out there. Good luck."

Leslie held Battle's nose in place long enough to drop a kiss on it. "Make us proud, boy. I know you can."

Leslie walked horse and jockey to a waiting escort pony and rider, handed over the lead shank, and then quickly crossed her fingers on both hands. They were going to need extra luck today.

They arrived at their seats in time to see Battlecry toe-dance his way through the post parade, but as soon as the field started their warm-up jog around the track, he seemed to settle a little. Leslie wouldn't relax, though, until he was safely in the gate and the race went off. Battle had the fifth post position in the nine-horse field, which pleased both Leslie and her father. Since Battlecry could act so badly in the gate, it was reassuring that he wouldn't be one of the first to load. And he wasn't so far outside that he'd be at a disadvantage.

Leslie trained her binoculars on the gate and held her breath. "Steady, boy," she whispered. Battlecry went in without too much of a fuss, and she sighed with relief. The other horses loaded. There was a moment of dead quiet, then the gate doors snapped open. The race was off!

Battlecry was out like a shot and for the first few strides was one of the horses fighting for an early lead. Karen was struggling to hold him back, slightly off the pace. One horse, Rubio, got his head in front along the rail, then moved to a length lead. Zinger settled just off him. Karen managed to place Battlecry behind and outside of Zinger, but he was fighting her and trying to pull himself forward despite her choking hold on the reins.

"Doesn't look like she's going to be able to pace him for long," Mr. D'Andrea muttered. "Let's hope she can save some of his speed."

"At least he's running." Leslie watched Karen work to hold Battlecry in third. "Zinger's jock can't be too happy," she said to her father. "I don't think they wanted to be so close to the pace."

"They didn't. They expected to chase our horse and Rubio until they burned themselves out."

Both stared silently at the field as they neared the end of the backstretch. The position of the first three runners hadn't changed, but they both could see that Battlecry wasn't going to put up with Karen's hold much longer. He was fighting her—

running with his head up, beginning to sweat, struggling to increase his speed.

"Okay, let him go!" Mr. D'Andrea said through clenched teeth. Karen seemed to be reading his mind. She gave the big horse rein, and instantly he settled and started pulling them forward. There would be no holding him now. He swept up on the outside of Zinger, coming on so quickly that Zinger's jockey was caught by surprise. In two strides, Battlecry roared past in hot pursuit of Rubio, who was weakening on the lead. Battle quickly put him away and was in the lead himself before the end of the far turn.

"Come on!" Leslie and her mother screamed with one voice. But the horse didn't need any encouragement. He surged into the stretch, gaining with every ground-eating stride.

"The long shot, Battlecry, has the lead!" the announcer shouted. "Dexter has set down Zinger for the drive and is going after him. Rubio is out of it. Wishful is making a strong move along the rail, working his way between horses. But the big black horse isn't going to be caught today. Karen Jenkins is hand riding him. She hasn't even lifted her whip, and he's still drawing away! They're coming down to the wire—and it's Battlecry, a decisive winner! Zinger four lengths back, then Wishful, closing in third. A real upset today. They said this horse was something, and he's certainly proved it! The black terror from nowhere wins the Nassau County Handicap in track-record-equaling time!"

"I don't believe it!" Leslie gasped. "I thought he might have a chance, but he crushed them! Dad, it's amazing."

Her father, with a smile from ear to ear, nodded, then added more soberly, "Don't forget he was carrying less weight than most of the field, and I think we caught Zinger's jockey totally by surprise. He wasn't expecting Battle to come up on him like that. Next time, they'll be prepared . . . if there is a next time."

The D'Andreas were mobbed on the way to the winner's circle. If people had paid attention to them before, now they were were really beseiged with questions. Battlecry preened before the cameras, tossing his dark head so his silky mane was flung high. Karen was laughing through tears of happiness. She'd pushed up her goggles, and someone handed her a towel to wipe the tears and flecks of track dirt from her face. The D'Andreas hurried up to her and Battlecry with their congratulations.

"Great ride," Mr. D'Andrea praised her. "I couldn't have asked for more."

"I was really worried I couldn't hold him long enough, and he sure let me know when he'd had enough. But I guess he still had plenty left."

"I guess!" Mr. D'Andrea laughed.

"You both did an incredible job." Leslie went to Battle's head and hugged him. "I knew you could do it. I'm so proud of you!"

Battle nickered, but quickly jerked his head free

as though the sentimentality embarrassed him. As Karen took her saddle to weigh in, more camera shutters clicked. Television crews had focused in force on horse and family, and commentators and reporters were waiting for their chance for interviews. A fresh saddle was placed on Battle's back, and Karen returned to remount for the official photos. Leslie stood proudly at Battlecry's head, with her parents close beside her. It was so amazing. All the cameras and attention left Leslie stunned. But Battlecry didn't have any qualms about being the star. He arched his neck, pricked his ears, and stared straight at the camera lens.

"You're such a ham," Leslie said with a chuckle when the photographers were done. She helped throw a satin sheet over Battlecry's back in preparation for taking him to the barn. A television commentator hurried up to her father with microphone in hand and cameramen following.

"So what are your plans for him now?" he asked with a smile. "Can we look for him again in the American Championship Racing Series? Another matchup with Zinger and Wishful?"

"I'll need time to catch my breath before I make any decisions," Mr. D'Andrea said. "We're coming into the series pretty late. I can see us heading toward the New England Classic and the Iselin Handicap, since they're here on the East Coast. I'm not sure about the Hollywood Gold Cup or the Pacific Classic. The purse he won today will help, but we're a small operation. This guy's the first

Grade 1 winner we've owned, and we certainly weren't expecting Grade 1 victories when we put him back in training," he said, laughing. "It's left me a little dazed."

"I understand you're planning on putting a portion of his winnings toward rescuing more retired racehorses."

"That's right. It's only fair, since he's a rescue horse himself."

"And what a horse he's turned out to be! We'll all be looking forward to seeing him again. A spectacular performance today. Congratulations!"

Battlecry seemed to understand. He threw up his head and gave a loud whinny. "Don't let it go to your head, big boy." Leslie smiled. "Come on, let's go back to the barn and get you settled and fed." But as she led him off, she was bursting with pride at the awed and admiring glances cast their way.

10

Leslie picked up the kitchen telephone on its first ring, listened, and then handed the phone to her mother. Since Battlecry had won the Nassau two weeks before, the phone hadn't stopped ringing. The racing papers were playing Battle's victory up big—a rags-to-riches story. Reporters kept calling to see if Mr. D'Andrea had made any decision about Battlecry's future schedule. Other racing fans were calling to find out more about the D'Andrea's rescue operation, wanting to contribute or take a look at the retrained Thoroughbreds that were for sale.

"You won't believe who that was." Mrs. D'Andrea gulped as she hung up the phone. "Amelia Whitley. You've heard of her."

Leslie nodded. The Whitley name was famous in racing. They ran one of the largest breeding and training farms in the country.

"She's sent us contributions before, but today she wanted to know if we're interested in selling Battlecry! She mentioned an incredible figure."

Leslie hadn't even thought about this happening, but she should have. Now that Battlecry had shown he had talent, very important people would be interested in owning him. "But we can't sell him!" she cried. "I'd die—and he'd hate it! He might go right back to his old habits without us!"

"Mrs. Whitley said she'd keep your father on as trainer. And the money, Les—it would sure help out."

"He'll be earning money for us. And if he stays good, there'll be stud fees!"

"We'd better go talk to your father."

Leslie's throat was tight as they walked out to the training stable. Her father was in one of the stalls, his tawny head bent low as he checked over a horse who'd bruised an ankle. Nick Bates was leaning on the wall outside, and Jeremy was inside the stall holding the horse's head.

"Phil," Mrs. D'Andrea said, "we need to talk."

"So talk. I'm listening."

Mrs. D'Andrea hesitated and glanced at Nick. "It's important."

"Pretend I'm not here," Nick said, grinning.

"Go ahead," her husband said. "What's up?"

"I just had the most amazing phone call from Amelia Whitley. They want to buy Battlecry. She offered half a million."

Mr. D'Andrea's head shot up. He stared at his wife. "You're serious?"

"Yes."

Slowly he stood up. "Half a million?"

Mrs. D'Andrea nodded.

Leslie could almost see the wheels turning in her father's mind. A half a million dollars was a lot of money—*much* more than they ever saw in a year. The money would make an incredible difference to her parents and the farm. But not to her, if it meant losing Battle!

"It's not enough," Nick said suddenly.

They all stared at him.

"He just won three hundred grand in the Nassau," Nick reasoned. "If you run him in a couple more of the American Championship races, and he gets even second- or third-place money, it'll put his winnings at over half a million."

"There's no guarantee that he'll do that well," Mr. D'Andrea said.

Nick grinned at him. "Always the pessimist. Come on, the way he's been running, he's bound to get up in the money. And then there's stud fees."

"I can't see them being much, with his bloodlines."

"The Whitleys don't offer half a million on a whim," Nick told him. "They must think he's a good stud prospect."

Mr. D'Andrea rubbed his chin and stared thoughtfully into space. "If I accept their offer now, it's money in the bank, even if he fails miserably from here on out."

Leslie went pale. This was a total nightmare. Her father was seriously considering selling Battle. Nick saw her expression.

"What do *you* think?" Nick asked her. "If it wasn't for you, the horse wouldn't be where he is now."

"I don't want to sell him," Leslie said quickly. She glanced nervously at her father. "I think he's worth more too."

"You do, huh?"

"So do I," Mrs. D'Andrea said firmly. Leslie looked at her gratefully.

Mr. D'Andrea wasn't giving in that easily. He leaned back against the stall partition.

"Why don't you give the guy a chance?" Nick pressed.

"I *have* given him a chance."

"Dad, you said just the other night that new people have been calling you, wanting you to train their horses," Leslie said. "All because of Battlecry."

Mr. D'Andrea closed his eyes and shook his head. A moment later he began to smile. "I'm outnumbered again!"

"We'll keep him?" Leslie cried.

"I'll go with the majority."

Leslie yelped with joy and threw her arms around her father. "Thanks, Dad! You won't regret it, I promise."

"Smart move," Nick said.

"I hope you're right," Mr. D'Andrea answered. "That's a lot of money to whistle away."

"You'll make more," Nick said confidently. "Hey, Phil, you haven't told them the other news yet."

"What news?" Leslie and her mother asked.

"The vet was just here. Three of the mares are in foal, and Battlecry has to be the sire. Edwin noticed the mares were putting on weight."

"Foals?" Leslie gasped, trying to take it in. "Battle's sired three foals? From when he got in with the mares the first week we had him?"

"The timing seems right," her father said.

"I don't believe it. I'm so sorry, Dad. Are you angry?"

"Three months ago, I would have been furious. But the value of those foals has gone up a little since the stallion won the Nassau. So maybe it's not a complete disaster."

"Which mares?" Leslie asked.

"Good ones, fortunately. Vestin, Miss Tess, and Exotic Halo. They all have decent bloodlines, although they never did much at the track themselves."

"That terror knows how to pick his girlfriends, anyway," Jeremy said.

"So, it looks like you're in the breeding business, too." Nick grinned.

Mr. D'Andrea straightened up. "Whether we

want to be or not. That guy better keep winning races."

"I might be interested in taking a foal off your hands," Nick said. "Depending on how they turn out."

"You'll be paying a good price after what you talked me into today," Mr. D'Andrea shot back. "Oh, the other thing I was going to tell you," he added to Leslie and his wife, "I've gone ahead and entered him in the New England Classic in mid-July. The field shouldn't be as strong as the Nassau. He'll have a very decent chance of winning. We'll see how he does there before deciding on the California races."

Leslie and her mother exchanged a look. They were both smiling from ear to ear.

"It was awful!" Leslie told Adam the Sunday night after the New England Classic. As soon as they'd gotten home from New Hampshire early that evening, she'd called him, and he'd come over to hear the story. They sat on the patio behind the farmhouse, sipping cold drinks. Even at dusk it was sweltering, still over eighty degrees and humid, without a hint of a breeze. It hadn't been any cooler in New Hampshire that weekend, either.

"He seemed okay in the morning," Leslie said, "but he got worse all day long. He wouldn't even settle down when I was with him. By the time we got him to the walking ring, he was absolutely crazy: covered in sweat, rearing up. I haven't seen him that nuts since he was in the auction ring."

"Maybe the heat got to him," Adam suggested. "And you must have been mobbed by reporters."

"Yeah, we were. But wait till you hear the rest." Leslie could see the whole horrible scene replaying in front of her eyes, and felt sick. "We managed to get Karen in the saddle—and that wasn't easy. He calmed down a little during the post parade and warm-up, but as soon as they lined up to go into the gate, he went wild. He tried to go after Wishful and take a chunk out of his neck. The gate assistants pulled him away, but it took four of them to get him in the gate. And then"—Leslie swallowed and shook her head—"as they were loading the last horse . . . Battle reared up in the gate! I thought for a minute he was going to go right over backward. I was so scared for Karen! She managed to hang on—I don't know how. Battle burst right through the front door of the gate. A couple of exercise riders came around and helped Karen get him under control. But, of course, they scratched him from the race."

"I'm really sorry," Adam said, taking Leslie's hand.

"My father's face was absolutely white. I suppose mine was too. It was so embarrassing. I mean, if you'd heard what the reporters and other trainers had to say afterward! 'Can't teach an old dog new tricks . . . back to his old ways.' That kind of stuff. And they were right—he was acting just like he did when Hawkins trained him. Uncontrollable."

Adam was silent for a minute, rubbing the back of Leslie's neck. "What's your father going to do?" he asked quietly.

"We don't have much choice. When they finally got him off the track, we saw that his right foreleg was bleeding. He'd gashed it below the knee. Probably caught it when he reared up in the gate."

"Is it serious?"

"No, but he'll have to stay quiet for a few weeks until it heals. It's my father I'm worried about. He hardly said two words all the way home. Remember, we had just talked him into turning down half a million dollars for Battlecry. We were so sure he'd be winning more races, and his stud value would be going up. But after the way he behaved this weekend—" Leslie's voice caught in her throat, and she leaned her head on Adam's shoulder.

"It's too soon to think that," Adam said soothingly. "Something must have upset him. He'll behave again after this."

"I hope so . . . I really hope so." Leslie buried her face in her hands, and Adam slid closer to put his arms around her shoulders.

Mr. D'Andrea was grim and somber the entire week after the New England Classic. Leslie overheard him on the phone with a reporter who'd called the farm. "He's definitely out of the West

Coast races. No, I have no explanation for his be-havior. Aside from a cut on his leg, which will heal, he's fit. We'll rest him a few weeks and see what happens. Yes, the Iselin Handicap Labor Day weekend is still a possibility . . ."

Battlecry was only slightly subdued after his hair-raising performance. His leg was obviously sore, so he took it easy on his own, but his attitude was just as arrogant as ever. When Leslie was in the stall, talking to him, grooming him, and check-ing his bandage, he showed no signs of remorse.

"I wish you could talk," Leslie sighed to him, "and tell me what was bothering you that day."

Battlecry snorted, tore a mouthful of hay from his net, and looked at her.

"You're not tired of racing, are you?"

The big horse tossed his head, though Leslie was sure he didn't actually understand her words. He must have known she was upset, though, from the tone of her voice. He nudged his velvety nose against her shoulder, then immediately went back to his feed.

Edwin had come up to the stall door in time to hear Leslie's last words. "I wouldn't give up on him yet," the old man said. "I don't think he's had his fill of racing."

"I feel like he's going backward. He hasn't acted this badly since Hawkins had him."

"Horses have their moods, just like people. My guess is that all the excitement got to him. Four big races in two months, with a lot of people gawking at him. He isn't used to that. It sent him over the edge. I've seen it before," Edwin added, rubbing his chin. "He had a little something he had to get out of his system. He's got it out, and you've got the right touch to get him back on track."

Leslie respected Edwin's experienced advice, yet she had real fears that Battle had turned himself around again—the wrong way.

"How are the mares doing?" she asked, to change the subject.

"Oh, good—real good. I expect we'll have some youngsters around here in January. They'll be fine looking, too, with a sire like him."

"I think I'll go out and have a look at them," Leslie said.

Edwin walked with her to the pasture, and together they studied the three mares Battlecry had chosen. They were all handsome, nicely conformed animals. One was gray, another chestnut, and the third, Exotic Halo, was as black as Battlecry himself. "I wonder who the foals will look like," Leslie mused.

"Don't be surprised if they take after their sire." Edwin nodded decisively. "Yup. In temperament, too. He's what I call a dominant stallion."

As they walked back to the barn, Leslie's mother and Nick came toward them up the drive. Mrs. D'Andrea was dressed for riding; she was schooling some of the new rescue horses. Because of the heat, Nick had forsaken his battered tweed jacket and was in shirt sleeves.

126

Leslie hadn't seen Nick since the New England race. He came over and laid a hand on her shoulder. "Don't look so down in the dumps," he said. "The horse isn't finished yet."

"I think everyone's nerves are a little on edge," Mrs. D'Andrea told him. "Phil's been an absolute bear since the race."

"If he's upset about passing on the Whitley offer, then he should be upset with me, not you guys. Besides, I still think it was the right thing to do. Every horse is allowed one screwup. It's a shame, but he'll put his mind to it again."

"Go down and give Phil a pep talk," Mrs. D'Andrea suggested.

Nick laughed. "That's just where I was headed. Chin up, Les," he said in parting as he strode toward the training stable.

"You know, he's right," Mrs. D'Andrea said to Leslie. "Don't let your father's mood get to you. Keep believing in that arrogant horse. I do."

Mr. D'Andrea had taken Battlecry out of the training schedule for three weeks. It was brutally hot anyway, so it was just as well. Battle's cut had healed quickly, as the vet had promised. Within a week they could remove the bandages. For day-to-day care, Edwin gave Leslie a hand with the stallion. Leslie noticed with satisfaction that the big horse had taken to the old man. They understood each other, although Leslie was still the only human Battlecry trusted completely.

127

During the day, Leslie put Battlecry in the paddock, then walked him around the yard in the cooler evenings. She didn't want him losing his fitness and tone while he was out of serious training. Sometimes Adam came by and walked with them when he had a night off. Aside from Adam, Leslie hadn't seen much of her friends in the past month. Gabby had been away with her family for several weeks on vacation, but Kim hadn't been stopping by or calling like she usually did, and when they did talk, Kim sounded distant. Leslie knew she was partially to blame, because she'd been so busy with Battlecry, but still, it was strange.

"Have you seen Kim at all?" Leslie asked Adam as they led Battle along the drive one evening in mid-August. "When I call her, she always says she's busy."

"I've seen her in town, hanging around with Jared Rawson, riding on the back of his Yamaha."

"You're kidding! Still? But she's never even mentioned his name to me."

"I'm not surprised. She's probably afraid to. He's such a jerk—I know Kim's not the only girl he's going out with."

Leslie didn't know what to do. Should she say something to Kim? Would Kim get angry with her for butting in? Fortunately Gabby came home a few days later and stopped by the farm on her ten-speed. Gabby excitedly told Leslie all about her family's stay on Martha's Vineyard. "I met the cutest guys! One of them had a boat, and we all went sailing. . . . And guess what? I'm going for my driver's test next week. I'll be sixteen!"

Leslie's sixteenth birthday was still two months away, although she'd already applied for her driver's permit.

After Gabby had furnished all the details of her vacation in glowing color, Leslie asked, "Have you talked to Kim since you got back?"

Gabby scowled. "Yeah, I just saw her, as a matter of fact—down at Burger King. She was with that guy we saw her with at the beach party."

"Jared Rawson."

"She had her jeep parked next to his bike. She was practically hanging all over him, but he left without her."

"Did she see you?"

"Oh, yeah. I walked right over to her. I've been pretty angry because she hasn't wanted to do anything with me all summer. But get this—she told me she's madly in love. I tried to tell her Jared was a creep, but she wouldn't listen. It's weird! And I can't figure out why she thinks he's so great."

"Neither can I." Leslie frowned—she was really getting worried about Kim.

Leslie tried to call her several times in the next few days, but Kim was never home. Then Leslie had other things to think about: Battlecry was going back into serious training in preparation for the Iselin Handicap.

11

"Good, boy! Perfect!" Leslie praised the big horse a week later as they finished a half-mile breeze. Automatically, she rose in the saddle and started pulling him up. The heat wave had broken, and the August morning was surprisingly clear and comfortable. Battlecry certainly enjoyed the change in temperature. He sprang along over the dirt, tossing his head exuberantly. "Keep training like this, and my father will be in heaven," Leslie added with a smile as she firmly patted Battle's muscular neck. His performance was reassuring, but she couldn't forget that Battlecry had trained well before the New England Classic and had still gone to pieces the day of the race.

Mr. D'Andrea and Nick were both standing along the rail as Leslie rode Battle off the oval. Her father wasn't actually smiling, but he didn't look nearly as glum as he had a few weeks before. Nick, however, was beaming.

"Forty-five and a half seconds!" Nick called, holding up his stopwatch.

Leslie had guessed her fractions might be in that range. The time was excellent, especially considering the tight turns on her father's training track.

"That's half the problem solved," Mr. D'Andrea said. "The other half is to figure out how to keep him quiet the day of the race."

Leslie dismounted and pulled up the stirrups, giving Battle another well-deserved pat on the shoulder. He nickered his acknowledgment. "I had an idea about that," she said. In the last few days, she'd spent a lot of time thinking about it. "What if we wait and don't take him to Monmouth until the night before the race?" The New Jersey track where the Iselin Handicap would be run was only about an hour's drive from the D'Andrea farm.

Mr. D'Andrea scratched his cheek. "That occurred to me. He'd lose the chance to have a good work over the track before the race, but it might be worth it, if it keeps him from getting wired."

"You know," Nick suggested, "you could always take him over this week or next—just for the morning workout. He can get a feel for the track, and you can see how he handles the surface. Then bring him back here and let him settle down."

"That might work," Leslie said. Every track surface was slightly different in texture, depth, and composition, and seeing how Battlecry took to the Monmouth surface would help her father plan his strategy for the actual race.

"I could bring him over without a problem," Mr. D'Andrea mused. "Leslie could come and ride him for the workout." He nodded. "Okay. Let's try it. The race is in two weeks. We'll take him over in the middle of next week."

Battlecry knew something was up when Leslie loaded him in their one-horse van at four on Wednesday morning. The only time he rode in the van was when he was racing, but he didn't have time to work himself into a state. As soon as they'd parked on the backside of the Monmouth track, Leslie unloaded him, tacked him up, and she and her father led him directly to the track. Battlecry's head was up, with ears pricked forward. He flared his nostrils in growing excitement, but before he realized exactly what was happening, Leslie was in his saddle and was urging him through the gap onto the track. Mr. D'Andrea had already spoken to the officials and clockers, who were expecting the workout.

Leslie settled deep in the saddle, collected the reins, and forced the big stallion to keep his mind on business as she warmed him up. She also kept him clear of the other horses working on the track, and didn't move him in close to the rail until she was ready to gallop. Her father wanted a hard work, since this was the only one Battle would have on the track. She was to breeze Battle through a half mile, then gallop him out another three quarters. The Iselin was a mile and an eighth, so Battle would have worked the distance, and then some.

He performed like a dream, putting his heart and mind to it. Leslie knew their fractions were good, and so did Battle. As he strutted off the track, Leslie saw her father's satisfied expression— and a lot of other curious faces. She knew the others were wondering what Phil D'Andrea was up to, bringing the horse in for just one workout.

Only as Leslie stopped by her father's side and dismounted did Battle try any of his tricks. Leslie tried to remove his saddle, but he skittered around. He flung up his head and started prancing, pretending he was ready to show his handlers who was boss.

"Stop showing off," Leslie muttered to him as she finally pulled off the saddle. Then she held Battle's head, and her father threw a light sheet over Battle's back and fastened it. The horse's black coat was barely damp—a sign that the workout hadn't taken too much out of him.

"Let's cool him down and get out of here," Mr. D'Andrea said quietly. "I've been getting too many questions, and I'd rather keep our plans to ourselves."

Two hours later, they were back at the farm, and Battle was happily munching oats in his stall.

* * *

When Adam came by on his moped late that afternoon, he and Leslie saddled up a couple of the reconditioned horses and took a ride over to the beach. With Battlecry settled in his stall for the afternoon, Leslie had a couple of hours to herself. The crickets were chirping their late-summer song as they made their way to the beach, and the days had grown shorter, but there was still a warm breeze off the water.

"So the workout went well," Adam said.

"It was perfect, thank heavens!"

Adam looked over at her. "You sound like you're getting nervous about the race."

"I am. I'm just glad you're going to be coming with me."

Adam laughed. "I don't know how much help I'll be. I'll be pretty strung out myself."

"At least there'll be two of us. I'm terrified he'll act up again. And even if he doesn't, it'll be a much harder race for him. He'll be carrying more weight, and he only beat Zinger by three lengths last time."

"Yeah, but think of the good side—he's been training so well."

"Mmmm. We'll find out the morning of the race."

"Have you managed to get ahold of Kim?" Adam asked.

Leslie shook her head and frowned. "I've tried, but she's never there. Gabby hasn't heard from her either. It's really strange. She's being so dumb over that guy."

Leslie left the barn the afternoon before the Iselin after checking through Battle's tack box and giving him a good grooming. She had a lot on her mind. Her father would be vanning Battle to Monmouth that night, and Leslie was sure there were some last-minute things she'd forgotten.

Suddenly, she stopped in her tracks. Kim's red jeep was speeding up the driveway. She screeched to a halt a few feet from Leslie and jumped out. At first Leslie felt a wave of relief that Kim had come by, then she saw the expression on Kim's face. She looked awful—her normally perfect hair was rough and messy looking. Her face was pinched and white, except for swollen and red-rimmed eyes. And she looked like she had lost weight.

"What's wrong?" Leslie gasped, hurrying forward. "Kim, you look terrible!"

Kim seemed frantic. "Let's go to your room. I've got to talk."

Leslie quickly led the way inside and up the stairs to her bedroom. Fortunately Mrs. D'Andrea was out in the stables. Leslie shut the bedroom door. Kim paced across the room, then spun around and raised clenched fists to her mouth.

"I just saw Jared at the beach with Fiona Walsh! They were sitting on a blanket together. He had his arm around her—she was all pressed against him. Everybody was there—all Jared's friends!"

Leslie didn't know what to say. She remembered that Adam had told her that Jared went out with other girls. But obviously Kim hadn't known.

"We were supposed to go out today. He stood me up! For her!"

Leslie quickly put an arm around Kim's shoulders.

Kim stuttered hoarsely. "He . . . he saw me when I came down the beach. He didn't even care. He sort of shrugged and laughed, then, then one of his friends said, 'The kid's finally waking up.' They were all laughing at me! Oh, Leslie, I want to die!"

"Kim, I'm so sorry. How awful." She led Kim to her bed and sat her down.

"How could he! He knows how much I care about him." Kim's whole body shook as she started to sob hysterically. Between the sobs, she gasped out a story of arguments and broken dates. "I couldn't stand it anymore, Les. I started following Jared around . . . I had to see him . . ."

Leslie cringed to think that Kim had been that desperate.

"Someone hinted that he was fooling around with other girls—but I couldn't believe it. Then today I saw it with my own eyes! And he didn't care . . . he didn't care! I feel so awful! Oh, God, what am I going to do? I wish I were dead!" She buried her face in her hands.

Leslie tightened her grip on Kim's shoulders. "Kim, don't say that! Don't ever say that. Jared is a stupid jerk who isn't worth your time. He's a loser, and you're better off without him. Listen, there are other guys," Leslie said softly. "I know three or four guys who are dying to go out with you. Matt, and Jonas—"

"They're so young!" Kim cried. "Young and stupid! Like babies!"

"Is that why you're so crazy about Jared—because he's older?"

"No, of course that's not the only reason! He's cool, and has a great body. Any girl would be proud to be with him."

"Not me. Adam says he's bad news, always getting in trouble—" Leslie knew she'd made a mistake as soon as the words were out of her mouth.

"You've been talking about me!" Kim screeched. "And what would you know? You and Adam have never even gone out with anyone else! I bet he hasn't even kissed you," Kim sneered. "You don't know how I feel at all!"

Leslie was suddenly furious—Kim had no right to put down Adam. "Well, I sure don't understand the way *you've* been acting lately," she snapped back. "For the last month it's been Jared this and Jared that. You completely dumped me and Gabby!" Leslie took a deep breath. "Look, why don't you start riding again? Gabby said you've hardly ridden all summer."

"I sold Desert Sheik last week."

"You *what*?" Leslie gasped. That horse had

meant everything to Kim. She'd babysat for hours and hours to earn the money to buy him.

"Jared hated my riding. He said it was dumb."

"You sold your *horse* just because some stupid *guy* didn't like it?" Leslie exclaimed.

"Why are you making a big deal out of it? I was getting bored with riding anyway. I've outgrown it."

"Sure. You're one of the best riders on the Long Island circuit, and you'd rather ride on the back of a motorcycle with Jared!"

Kim jumped up and glared at Leslie. "No! I'm bored with it! That's all! I don't even know why I came over here. I thought you were my friend, but you obviously have no sympathy for me."

"I am your friend, and I do—"

"Forget it!" Kim stormed. "I should have talked to Gabby in the first place." Before Leslie could say another word, Kim had turned and raced out of the house. She was spinning her jeep down the drive by the time Leslie got to the front porch. She hurried back in the house and called Gabby. She felt sick; she shouldn't have yelled at Kim, but she'd lost her temper.

"I'll wait for her," Gabby said, after Leslie had filled her in. "I should have guessed something like this would happen. All because of that idiot, Jared. That guy really bites it."

"I know," Leslie agreed.

"By the way, good luck tomorrow."

"Thanks, Gab. Let me know what happens."

* * *

At five the next morning, Leslie, her mother, and Adam left the farm. During the drive down the Long Island Expressway toward New Jersey, Leslie told Adam about the scene with Kim. She'd been so worried that Kim would do something stupid, but Gabby had called back late in the afternoon to say that Kim was there and would be spending the night at Gabby's. Gabby had done what she could to calm Kim down.

Adam shook his head. "I never could figure how she got mixed up with him."

"Me either. I hope she's okay."

Once they arrived at the track, they put Kim's problems aside. The crowds and the press coverage were intense. Even at that early hour, television camera crews were setting up. Handicappers and press people roamed the barn area. When they met Mr. D'Andrea at Battlecry's stall, he was looking frazzled.

"Battle's being unbearable," he said. "He's only been here overnight, but he knows there's a race coming."

Emphasizing his words, a shrill whinny came toward them, and Leslie went over to the horse. He huffed dangerously, but allowed her to rest her hand on his gleaming neck. "Hey there, boy. I know. You're excited."

Leslie turned to her father. "Maybe he'd be better if we close his stall doors."

"You're right. He'll still hear the commotion, but at least it won't be in front of his eyes."

Battlecry did quiet down a little once she had closed the top stall door, but by early afternoon, Leslie had a lump in her stomach. Why did Battle always have to behave like this before a race? The steady stream of visitors who came by with a ton of questions for Leslie and her father didn't help her state of mind.

"So, you're expecting more fireworks?" one reporter asked with a sly grin as he eyed the closed stall.

"I'm expecting him to run a good race," Mr. D'Andrea said shortly.

"You kept him away from the track till the night before the race. That an indication of his condition?"

"The horse is fine."

"I see he clocked an incredible workout last week," another reporter remarked. "Zinger's people are looking at your horse as the one to beat. So why the mystery?"

Several people in the crowd laughed. "You wouldn't be asking that if you'd been up in New Hampshire and saw the show he put on before the New England Classic."

"Enough questions," Mr. D'Andrea said tersely. "I've got work to do."

The reporters gradually took the hint, but only after Adam and Mr. D'Andrea literally roped off the area near Battlecry's stall.

Karen came by to talk and get Mr. D'Andrea's thoughts about how the race would be run. Leslie gave her credit for her willingness to get in Battle's saddle again after he'd nearly gone over with her in the gate. Nick Bates arrived shortly before race time, smiling as usual. Yet there was an edge of worry under his air of confidence. "You've got them talking," he said to Mr. D'Andrea. "The bettors can't make up their minds about him. The odds are jumping all over the place."

"Personally, I don't blame them," Mr. D'Andrea told him. "I've got the worst case of nerves I've ever had in my career."

Leslie knew exactly how her father felt.

12

It was the New England Classic all over again! Leslie was sure the race was going to be a disaster. Battlecry was no sooner out of his stall than he broke into a sweat, marring Leslie's painstaking grooming job. It took both her and her father to get him to the saddling area. Then he reared while they were tacking him up. In the walking ring, he sashayed willfully and tried bucking Karen off when she mounted. Leslie heard the comments all around.

"He's going to blow it again."

"That guy's wired for sound. He'll never be able to run a decent race!"

Leslie felt the lump in her stomach turn hard and cold. A nervous sweat broke out on her forehead, and she felt sick. *Battle, get it together! Don't let me down!*

Karen's face was pale as the field headed for the

track, but she managed to get the stallion out there. The D'Andreas and Adam took their seats in the grandstand. Leslie reached over and took Adam's hand as the field finished their warm-up jog and headed toward the starting gate. Her fingers were ice cold.

"Please behave!" Leslie whispered. A second later she felt ready to cry, as Battlecry reared while being led to the gate. Karen was prepared this time, though. She stuck to him like a burr, hanging on to chunks of Battlecry's mane with her hands. Leslie knew what the jockey must be feeling.

"Battlecry showing his usual high spirits," the track announcer remarked. "But he's settling down now and going in."

"Sure," Mr. D'Andrea grouched, "with the help of four attendants."

Leslie didn't care how many attendants it took, as long as the horse was in. She saw one groom straddling the partition to take a firm grip on Battlecry's ear to prevent him from rearing. No one wanted to take any chances on his mood.

"Steady, steady," Leslie murmured. Her eyes were locked on Battle as the last horse loaded.

"And they're off!" the announcer cried.

Nine horses shot from the gate. Battlecry jumped out jerkily, and was a stride behind the rest as they thundered away from the gate. It took another few strides before Karen was able to settle the big stallion and get his mind to business. By then, the rest of the field was ten lengths ahead.

"He's lost it," Leslie whispered miserably. Yet as she watched the horses surging down the backstretch, she saw Battlecry was making up incredible ground. With huge, ground-eating strides, the black horse started catching horses and putting them away!

"Finally he's concentrating," Mr. D'Andrea muttered.

Karen was weaving Battle through the pack, trying to save ground, and as they came into the far turn, he was amazingly up into fourth along the rail with only Zinger and two tiring speed horses in front of him. But they were lengths in front.

Leslie couldn't seem to catch her breath. Her pulse roared in her ears, and she knew she was going to faint. Adam squeezed her cold hand, but she barely felt the pressure. So much depended on this race.

"He's not going to be able to do it," Leslie groaned.

"Shhh," Adam said. "Give him a chance."

Battlecry roared past one tiring horse, then the other, into second, and with each stride he was shortening the distance between himself and Zinger. Suddenly, Leslie saw Wishful putting in his usual late run, sweeping up on the outside of the field. Zinger's jockey looked back over his right shoulder and saw Wishful coming too. As they came off the turn into the stretch, Zinger's jockey asked him for more speed. But the jockey hadn't looked to his left to see Battlecry coming up on his inside.

They were at the eighth pole when Battlecry slipped through the narrow opening along the rail to pull up stride for stride with Zinger. Zinger's jockey went desperately for his whip, but Battlecry wasn't going to give an inch.

Leslie dazedly heard the track announcer's soaring voice. "A paint-scraping ride by Karen Jenkins! Battlecry is showing his true mettle today. Unbelievable, the ground this horse has made up! Battlecry on the rail. Zinger fighting back outside. Nose and nose . . . neither giving an inch! Wishful four lengths back in second with no hope of catching them. At the sixteenth pole, they're still nose and nose. The horse race everyone's been waiting for! And they're under the wire! It's too close to call! Photo finish!"

"You've just seen the performance of a lifetime," Mr. D'Andrea said to the others. "For him to make up that kind of ground and still hold on! He was carrying equal weight, too."

Leslie gulped. "I'm feeling kind of dizzy."

Adam quickly took her arm as they headed down to the winner's circle. The infield board was lit with the word PHOTO. They wouldn't know who actually had crossed under the wire first until the judges had examined the photo. Karen was riding Battlecry back down the track. He was putting on a show for the spectators, but Leslie could see the race had taken much more out of him than his

145

previous races. His gleaming black coat was marred by patches of lathered sweat. Leslie and her father hurried up to horse and rider.

"I'm amazed," Mr. D'Andrea said to the jockey. "I never thought you'd get up there after that lousy start. How'd you see the finish?"

"I thought we had him," Karen answered breathlessly. "In another stride, we definitely would have. But I'm not sure."

"Incredible job."

Karen rubbed her hand along Battlecry's sweaty neck. "You'd better give him the credit. I just steered and hung on for the ride. He did the rest all by himself."

Leslie held Battlecry as Karen dismounted and removed the saddle for her weigh-in. "You're really something," Leslie whispered to the horse as she walked him in a circle. "I don't think you realize how special you are—even if you just about give everyone heart failure before a race." Battlecry bobbed his head as she patted his sweat-drenched neck. "What do you think, Dad?" Leslie added. "He looks pretty tired."

Mr. D'Andrea had been carefully studying the horse. "He's moving all right. We'll know more when we get him back to the barn. To be safe, I'll have the vet look him over."

The infield board still read PHOTO, and the crowd of spectators jammed along the grandstand rail waited expectantly. Except for Zinger, who was being walked a few yards away, the other horses

146

in the field were being led off by their grooms. Leslie saw television crews aiming their cameras at Battlecry and Zinger. Commentators and reporters waited for a decision and the opportunity for interviews. Leslie's stomach was knotted with tension. She looked over at her mother and Adam, who were standing by the rail. They both smiled their encouragement. She smiled back, but her mouth felt stiff.

Then, at last, the track announcer's voice boomed over the loudspeakers. "The judges have made a decision. Battlecry wins it by a fraction of a nose! A remarkable finish to the American Championship Racing Series—a stirring stretch drive that won't soon be forgotten. Battlecry's proved himself to be in the ranks of the top-rated horses in the country!"

A spontaneous and heartfelt cheer went up from the crowd. "Battlecry, way to go!" someone yelled.

Leslie looked at her father. "They really like him," she gasped.

"I think he's become a kind of folk hero," her father said, smiling. From his expression, Leslie could tell he hadn't quite taken in the victory. But now the rest of the ceremonies could proceed. Battle went into the winner's circle. Television crews zoomed in, and commentators moved between the D'Andreas and Zinger's owners and trainer, who came over to shake hands with the D'Andreas. Adam went to Leslie's side.

"This is something!" he breathed. "How are you feeling?"

"Excited—but kind of numb," Leslie said.

"Yeah, I can imagine. I'll walk with you when you take him back to the barn."

"Please. My father and mother will have to stay for the presentation. Okay, big boy, let's go," she said to Battlecry. "You're ready for a nice, cool bath, I'll bet." Together she and Adam walked Battlecry toward the backside. Spectators waved and cheered as they passed. Battlecry wasn't too tired to preen and eye his admirers. Leslie still felt dazed. It just wasn't sinking in. She needed to get away from the crowds and the noise and quietly absorb Battlecry's feat.

There were more calls of congratulations in the barn area, but Leslie heard them with only half an ear as she and Adam led Battlecry out into the yard near his stall. The groom who'd been helping Mr. D'Andrea had a bucket, sponges, and drying cloths waiting. He and Adam held the stallion as Leslie sluiced water over Battlecry's sweaty back. The horse gave a grunt of pleasure.

"Feels good, doesn't it, boy?" Leslie said as she washed away the sweat and track dirt. "You deserve it. You deserve the best of everything." When he was clean, and Leslie had toweled him off, she and Adam led the horse along the paths under the trees to finish cooling him out. With the excitement over, Battlecry was beginning to show the extent of his tiredness. His head drooped slightly as they walked, and he showed no signs of his normal fiery spirit. He did lift his head to return the call of a stabled horse, but he was almost docile as they finished walking him and led him back to his stall.

Not long after Leslie had settled the stallion inside, the track vet walked over. "Hi, I'm John Finch," he said. "Your father asked me to look him over. How'd he seem?"

"Pretty tired."

Leslie watched, feeling a tinge of uneasiness, as Dr. Finch went in to examine Battlecry. Yet fifteen minutes later when he stepped back outside, he seemed satisfied.

"He looks fine to me—tired, but that's not surprising after the race he just ran. You've got an outstanding racehorse here. See how he eats, and let me know if any other problems develop." He headed off down the barn to check another horse.

Leslie filled Battlecry's feed bucket and was glad to see the stallion go straight to it. But he only sniffed and lipped up a mouthful, then he lost interest.

Adam laid a hand on Leslie's arm. "He'll be okay. Just wait till tomorrow."

"I guess. But he's never been like this before."

"He's never raced a race like that before either."

Leslie let herself out of the stall, and a moment later her parents hurried up. "Sorry it took us so long," her mother said. "We were mobbed by reporters. How is he?"

"The vet says fine, but he's not eating."

Mr. D'Andrea had already gone into the stall and was checking the horse over himself. "He looks okay physically. He should be a lot more perky by morning. Let's watch him for another hour, then I think we all deserve a celebration dinner! I asked Karen to join us."

Leslie realized she was exhausted. It felt almost like she'd run the race herself. But everyone else was keyed up as they set out to a nearby restaurant.

"I can't believe all the excitement Battlecry's creating," Mrs. D'Andrea said when they were all sitting around a table. They'd asked for a quiet corner table, but they'd been recognized by racegoers in the crowd, who looked over with smiles. It was all very strange to Leslie, and she knew her parents felt the same. "Everyone's just astounded at the race he put in," her mother continued. "Especially after the way he behaved beforehand. And Zinger's owners are already talking to us about a match race! They want to see the two of them match up in the Breeder's Cup Classic."

"What do you think about that, Dad?" Leslie asked.

"Until now, I hadn't, though it's only two months away. It seems like a logical step, but he was never nominated. We'd have to pay supplemental fees."

"With a clean trip, he could win it," Karen said. "Anyone who watched this race knows he's far and away the better horse. I mean the way he overcame that bad start and fought his way to the front! You should have heard the other jockeys!" Karen grinned. "Were they ever impressed!"

"Then how come you don't have a date tonight?" Adam teased.

Karen winked at him. "Tomorrow."

"And how many other trainers have been offering you rides?" Mr. D'Andrea asked with a smile.

"A few." Karen blushed. "But I'm loyal! You guys came first. You gave me my big chance."

"I wasn't worried about that."

"You know," Karen added, "if he won the Classic, they might consider him for older horse of the year honors."

"No," Mr. D'Andrea said. "He hasn't run enough races. Zinger would be the logical choice, even if we beat him again."

"But still." Mrs. D'Andrea sighed. "Seven months ago, who would have thought we'd even be talking about it?"

Leslie helped to unload Battlecry from the van on his return to the farm the next day and immediately knew something was wrong. Instead of nipping out at Jeremy and making everyone's life miserable, he followed her like a lamb to his stall. Edwin had come out to help with the unloading and noticed too. He shook his head and frowned.

"Looks feverish to me."

Mr. D'Andrea followed them into the barn. "I'm

calling the vet. He hasn't been coming back the way he should, and he does seem feverish. He may have a low-grade infection. What do you think?" he asked Edwin.

The old man fingered his chin and nodded. "Maybe picked up a bug at the track."

"Could it be serious?" Leslie asked.

"Don't worry," her father said. "If it is an infection, I'm sure he'll be fine once we get him on some antibiotics. This guy's a powerhouse physically."

Leslie ran her hand over Battlecry's sleek back. He nickered and made an effort to crane his head around, but he wasn't even mildly playful. "You really don't feel good, do you?" Leslie said. She leaned her head against his neck and put her arms around him. "Poor guy. We'll get you all fixed up. Don't worry."

Leslie stayed by the stall as their regular vet checked Battlecry over. "Definitely has a fever," he said. "Has he been eating?"

"Sort of."

"I'll start him on antibiotics and get some blood samples tested, but otherwise he looks okay. While I'm here, do you want me to check over those mares?"

"Might as well," Mr. D'Andrea said. "Edwin's been keeping a close eye on them, but I'd rather be on the safe side—especially now. Those foals are going to be a pretty valuable investment."

The vet chuckled. "You've changed your mind a little since last spring."

"I sure have." Mr. D'Andrea smiled. "I was ready to geld him back then—and a couple of times since."

"Be glad you didn't. He'll have plenty of good breeding years ahead of him."

School started the next day. It seemed like the summer had flown by, but now Leslie had to start her junior year of high school. It felt strange to be so old suddenly—she would be sixteen pretty soon. This year would be the junior prom, not to mention the homecoming dance.

Leslie hated leaving Battlecry for hours on end while he was sick, but Edwin said he'd check on him while she was gone. Over the next few days, she spent what free time she had in the afternoons in his stall, but in the mornings, she was still helping her father with workouts and had to rush off to school afterward.

Edwin and Jeremy kept a careful guard on the barn, since visitors had started arriving unexpectedly at the farm to see Battlecry. He really had become a folk hero, but the last thing the stallion needed was a flock of curious people gaping over his stall door. Leslie and her mother set up a bulletin board of clippings recording Battlecry's brief but dramatic career, and the visitors had to be satisfied with that.

The antibiotics were helping. Blood tests had

confirmed that Battle had a low-grade infection. By the end of the week, his fever was gone, but he was far more docile than usual. Seeing Battle subdued and quiet was more of a worry to Leslie than seeing him ready to kick out his stall. The effort he'd put forth in the Iselin really had worn him out.

"Hey," Jeremy told her, "enjoy the peace while it lasts. Another week, and he'll be screaming to get out and trying to take a chunk out of Edwin or me."

"I liked him better when he was giving everyone a hard time."

Jeremy rolled his eyes. "You've never been on the wrong end of his hindquarters."

A few minutes later Leslie heard voices at the end of the barn. She looked over the stall door, ready to warn off any intruders, but she saw Kim and Gabby coming down the barn aisle. "Well, hi!" she called. Since their argument, Leslie had hardly seen Kim at all, even at school, and was sadly beginning to fear their long friendship was over.

"Jeremy said it was all right for us to come in," Gabby said.

"Yeah, sure. It's just the strangers we're trying to keep away."

"How is he?"

"Getting better, though it's taking longer than I expected."

Battlecry had come to the stall door and pushed

his head over to see what was going on. When he saw the two girls, he snorted and flattened his ears.

Leslie laid a quieting hand on his muzzle. "You know Kim and Gabby. Just take it easy."

Kim shifted uneasily, then spoke to Leslie in a rush. "I came over because I wanted to tell you how sorry I am for getting mad at you. I know I was being a jerk, and you were only trying to help," she said. "But I was just feeling so hurt—"

Leslie interrupted her. "You don't have to apologize. I said some things I shouldn't. I've been feeling pretty bad myself. How are you doing these days?"

"Okay," Kim said, sighing. "I'm not seeing Jared anymore. I guess I was acting pretty crazy over him. I'm starting to see that he wasn't so great after all. He came over two nights ago, and I told him off." She gave a watery grin. "I felt a lot better afterward."

"Good," Leslie said with a smile. "You really are too nice for him, and there are tons of other guys."

"Matt already asked me to go to the movies tomorrow night. He and I are just friends," Kim quickly added, "but that's all I want right now."

"Are *we* good friends again?" Leslie asked.

"Of course!" Kim cried. "I mean, if you want to be. I think I've been feeling worse about *our* fight than I have about Jared."

"I want to be." Kim reached out, and the two girls hugged each other fiercely. Leslie's eyes felt

155

misty. She'd been more upset about Kim than she'd realized.

"We're going riding at the beach tonight," Gabby said cheerfully. "We thought maybe you and Adam would like to come."

"Sure!" Then Leslie looked at Kim. "But I thought you sold Desert Sheik."

"The girl who bought him broke her arm—not riding. She asked me to look after him and keep him in action. I've been training him again for the fall events."

"All right!" Leslie laughed. "I'm so glad you're going to be riding again. You're too good to quit! I'll call Adam. He can take one of our horses. What time do you want to go?"

"Right after dinner. Gabby and I will meet you here, okay?"

"Okay!"

When Kim and Gabby left, Leslie was feeling more cheerful than she had in weeks. Now, if Battle would only get back in shape quickly. Turning to Battlecry, she gave him a hug too. He wouldn't have tolerated it from anyone else, but he only whickered. "You big sweetheart," Leslie said, sighing. "Please, get better soon."

When Leslie went to the house to call Adam, her parents were standing in the kitchen talking. "I'd better tell you the news too," her father said. "Nick's talked me into supplementing Battlecry to the Breeder's Cup Classic. It's not every day that a horse like this comes along. He's sure been a god-send for me—for all of us."

Mrs. D'Andrea laughed. "You mean, when he wasn't giving you the king of all headaches?"

Her husband smiled. "Of course, it depends on how he comes back from this infection. I won't race him if there's the slightest hint he isn't one hundred percent fit. But we've got two months. If all goes well, we'll put him back in training early next month."

Leslie gave her father a high sign. "Sounds good to me."

13

During September, Leslie wasn't surprised at the growing air of excitement and anticipation on the farm. Everyone felt it. Breeder's Cup Day was the most important in the racing year. The Kentucky Derby received more attention, but it was a single race, restricted to three-year-olds. There were seven Breeder's Cup races—Juvenile Colts, Juvenile Fillies, the Sprint, the Mile, the Distaff, the Turf, and the three-million-dollar, mile-and-a-quarter Classic. The races attracted the very top horses from both sides of the Atlantic. For the first time in Phil D'Andrea's career, he would have a horse running in one of the races.

"I just don't believe it," Jeremy told Leslie as she put Battlecry in the paddock one late-September afternoon. "That monster actually made it to the big time. I would have bet every penny I have that he'd flop."

"Good thing you didn't," Leslie said, grinning.

"He's still a holy terror, though. Nothing will change my mind about that."

"I like him just the way he is," Leslie said firmly.

Battlecry looked up from his grazing and vigorously nodded his elegant head. Leslie laughed, but Jeremy shook his own head and walked away.

Yet as pleased as Leslie was to see Battlecry recovering from his infection, she knew he wasn't one hundred percent, and if he was going to be ready for the Breeder's Cup, he'd have to go back into training soon. The races were the first weekend in November.

"Have a little patience," Edwin told her. "He's coming along just fine. If you push him back into training too soon, it'll do more harm than good."

"I know. Dad says the same thing. I'm just getting so excited!"

"Aren't we all!" Edwin laughed.

Edwin did what he could to help Leslie and speed along Battlecry's recovery. While Leslie was at school, he walked the stallion and started working him lightly on the longe line. He helped Leslie in the barn, too, mucking out Battle's stall and cleaning his tack. The one thing he didn't do was groom the stallion; Battlecry would have put up a fuss. Leslie was still the only one from whom the horse allowed any intimacy.

"He's formed a bond with you," Edwin told Leslie one evening. It had rained earlier, but Leslie had taken a well-sheeted Battlecry out despite the weather. Knowing how stressed he got when he didn't exercise enough, Leslie had decided to take him out. Edwin walked along with them. Battle paused every so often to nibble the lushest blades of grass under the dripping trees.

"See how relaxed he is?" Edwin said. "I couldn't take him out alone and have him this calm, and he likes me better than most."

"He wouldn't be this calm if we were at the track," Leslie reminded him.

"Yeah, but if someone had cared for him and loved him early on the way you're doing now, I don't think this guy would have been as unsettled as he is now. That horse loves you," Edwin said.

Pleasure flushed Leslie's cheeks. Battle's love was more important to her than his winning races. "I love him too."

"Even more important, he trusts you."

Leslie's jaw set in a firm line. "And I trust him too."

By early October, when Battlecry was due to go back in training, he still showed a certain listlessness. He stood placidly while Leslie tacked him up and followed her like a lamb out to the training oval.

Mr. D'Andrea frowned when he saw them. The stallion's willing obedience was definitely out of character. "Hmph. He's not himself yet, is he? I think we'll just work him at a walk and a trot the next few days, gradually build him up. But he's been eating okay?"

"Yup. His appetite's completely back."

"Good sign. And don't look so discouraged," her father added. "He'll snap back. This is normal. It just takes time."

Leslie forced herself to stay optimistic, and each day Battle did seem more alert and slightly more frisky. They slowly increased his training regimen and started working him at a light jog on the track. But he had little of his normal fire and spark of mischief.

"He's put meat back on his bones," Edwin told her encouragingly when he found Leslie outside Battle's stall, looking and feeling depressed. "And look at that nice shine in his coat."

"I know. I guess I just expected him to bounce right back."

"Just wait."

Then, on an especially crisp October morning, Battlecry charged out of his stall, snorting and huffing in excitement. He toe-danced out to the oval and immediately craned his neck to try to nip one of the other horses.

Leslie looked over and saw her father's delighted grin. "Here we go," he said, beaming. "He's back in form. Let's make the most of it!"

"Looks like we're going to Florida!" Leslie cried when she saw her friends later that morning at school.

"He's back in shape again, huh?" Adam smiled. "Finally! Maybe the colder weather woke him

161

up, but he was like a different horse this morning —a real terror. It's wonderful!"

Kim and Gabby each gave Leslie a hug. "You're going too, aren't you?" Kim asked.

"You better believe it. How could I miss Battle running in the Breeder's Cup Classic? Mom and Dad said I could take a few days off. The race is too important, and Dad needs me there to keep Battle in line. I'm so excited! It's going to be so incredible!"

"Boy, I wish I could go," Gabby groaned. "I'd rather not be around when my parents see this quarter's report card."

"I thought you were getting extra help in algebra," Kim exclaimed.

Gabby wrinkled her nose. "Well . . . I kind of missed going a few times."

They all shook their heads at her. "I'll give you a hand," Adam offered. "You've still got some time before the end of the marking period."

Over the next week and a half, Battlecry's training intensified. To build up his stamina, Leslie rode him for long jogs around the oval, and she and her father took him over to the now deserted beach for a gallop on the sand. That outing was as much playtime as work for Battle as he chased after the waves and danced through the shallow water, showing his delight with a pleased toss of his head.

By the end of the week, they'd moved on to

short breezes, and everyone on the farm was there to watch.

"He looks fantastic!" Leslie's mother cried as Leslie rode off the track and dismounted after an excellent breeze. Mrs. D'Andrea gave her daughter a hug, then quickly gave Battlecry a pat on the neck as he snorted indignantly at being ignored. "Yes, you deserve some praise too. I know you're going to make us all very proud. What do you think?" she said to her husband.

"I don't like counting chickens before they're hatched, but there's a good possibility of his doing well. That is, if he keeps his act together until he's out of the gate."

That Friday night Adam picked up Leslie after dinner, proudly showing off his new used Mustang. He'd finally saved up enough money to buy it from the neighbor. As Leslie climbed in, he patted the car fondly. "What do you think?"

"It's great," Leslie said, smiling.

"I still have a lot of work to do on it. There's some rust, and I need to fix the upholstery, but the engine runs like a charm," Adam said enthusiastically. Leslie started to understand how Adam must feel when she went on about horses all the time.

"Where are you going?" she asked in confusion a few minutes later as Adam wove down some side streets. "I thought we were going to the movies."

"Slight change of plan." Adam smiled mysteriously.

"Oh?" Leslie frowned as Adam drew over to the curb on a residential street. "But this is Gabby's house."

"Yeah, she wanted us to stop by for a second. She wouldn't say why."

Leslie shrugged. "Maybe she wants to go with us. I should have asked her. I know Kim has a date tonight."

"We'll see." They climbed the steps to the front door and rang the bell. Almost instantly Gabby opened the door.

"Hi, guys. Come on in for a sec," she said, motioning them toward the darkened living room.

Suddenly the lights flashed on, and two dozen kids jumped up and yelled "SURPRISE!"

Leslie's mouth fell open. Her sixteenth birthday was the next day, and she and Adam had made plans to go out to a fancy restaurant then to celebrate. She hadn't expected this! "Oh, my gosh," she cried. "Oh, you guys!"

"Well, don't just stand there!" Kim laughed. "It's your party. The seat of honor is right here!"

Adam put his arm around Leslie's waist and led her forward. A table was piled with presents, and another was laden with food and drinks. Streamers were draped from the ceiling. Someone started the tape deck.

"This is unreal," Leslie said. "You've done so much!"

"You deserve it," Gabby said, grinning. "Not only are you turning sixteen and can finally get your license—but you're turning into a celebrity. After the Breeder's Cup, you and Battle are going to be stars!"

Leslie sighed happily. "Thanks, guys! You're great!"

From the rail at Gulfstream Park, Mr. D'Andrea signaled Leslie to start Battlecry's gallop. It was the last day in October, and they'd left Long Island with crisp temperatures and leaves that were a blaze of crimson and gold. Florida was hot and muggy—unseasonably hot even for that climate.

Leslie's shirt already felt sticky from sweat as she crouched lower in the racing saddle, gave Battlecry more rein, and clucked in his ear. Battlecry had been waiting for the signal and shot off in a ground-eating gallop.

"Good boy," Leslie murmured, feeling a huge wave of relief.

Leslie knew their fractions were good as they pounded around the oval, and she still had Battlecry under a slight hold, waiting for the last quarter mile to let him all the way out. They came off the far turn. She saw the quarter pole, kneaded her fisted hands along Battlecry's neck, and he flew toward the wire. As they passed under, she stood in her stirrups and drew back on the reins. Battlecry obstinately shook his head, at first resisting her restraint, but gradually he dropped back to a canter. "That's my boy!" Leslie praised. "What a super workout!" The stallion arched his neck as she turned him and rode off the oval to where her father, Nick Bates, and Jeremy were standing. The workout definitely made up for Battlecry's earlier behavior. He'd been so willful when she'd first ridden him out on the track that Leslie had been afraid he'd never settle down. But as she left the oval, her father and Nick Bates were both smiling.

"Nice job!" Nick called. "Real good clocking for that last quarter."

"I see you had a tough time getting him to settle," Mr. D'Andrea added, "but he's barely blowing."

Leslie dismounted with a smile and hugged Battlecry's neck before removing his saddle. He danced sideways at the end of the rein, full of high spirits. *It's so good to have him acting like himself again!* Leslie thought. She managed to slide the saddle off, and Jeremy came over to collect it. "He's not sweating much, either," she said as she ran her hand over the horse's back.

"So I see." Her father nodded. "The heat doesn't seem to be bothering him. I was afraid it might. We'll give him a light jog tomorrow and Saturday, and he should be ready to go."

"When's Karen coming in?" Leslie asked.

"This afternoon. I'll let her take him out for one of the jogs so they can get reacquainted. And your mother will be here tonight. Getting excited?" he asked with a teasing grin.

"Yeah. And nervous."

"It'll be a piece of cake," Nick said confidently. "Even the handicappers are backing him to the hilt. He'll go in the race as favorite."

Mr. D'Andrea rubbed his chin. "It may be superstitious, but I don't like going in as a favorite."

"Well, it'll make for a change anyway." Nick laughed. "What was he in the Nassau—50 to 1? And at least 15 to 1 in the Iselin."

"Because the bettors were afraid he'd act up in the gate again."

Nick looked behind them and motioned with his head. "Here they come."

Leslie saw several reporters approaching.

"Let's get moving," her father said. "I'm not in the mood for questions this morning."

"Better get in the mood," Nick answered. "They're not going to leave you alone."

Nick was right. Leslie was dazed by the attention they received over the next days. She was interviewed; her father and mother were interviewed. Even Jeremy was asked for his comments. Every time Leslie took Battlecry out of his stall, a photographer seemed to be waiting, and Battlecry was doing everything in his power to live up to his notorious reputation. He knew something very big was coming, and he was ready to terrorize any stranger who came near his stall.

"THE TERROR IS MAKING HIS PRESENCE KNOWN," read one racing headline.

Of course, there was plenty of speculation in the racing papers and among the backside staff that Battlecry would blow his chances again with his prerace behavior. He was still considered unpredictable by most. There was some question, too, that his brief illness had taken a toll on him. But one look at the high-minded stallion was enough to tell anyone that he was in top physical form.

On Saturday morning a call came through to the barn from Adam, Kim, and Gabby, wishing Leslie good luck. "We'll be glued to Gabby's television," Adam told her. "We'll videotape it for you."

"Thanks, guys. I'm so glad you called. I'm getting so nervous I can't think straight. And I miss you."

"I miss you too. But don't worry—he'll do great. Your fan club up here's cheering."

After she'd hung up, Leslie went back to Battlecry's stall. He was quieter when she was around, and she needed to give him a special grooming. Battlecry cocked his head as Leslie tried to talk away her case of nerves. "I know you'll beat him," she said, "but please try to behave a little better at the gate today. You blew one race and *almost* blew another by acting so crazy and not paying attention."

Battlecry snorted indignantly. "Well, you did! And Karen's going to be uptight anyway. This is the biggest race of her life. The biggest race of *your* life, too."

Battlecry rubbed the side of his head against her shoulder, scratching an itch.

"Amazing!" someone gasped.

Leslie jumped at the sound of the voice behind her. Battlecry picked up his head and gave an angry grunt. Leslie turned to see a youngish man in a cotton sports shirt with a press badge pinned to his pocket.

"Stay back from the stall," she warned quietly.

"Oh, I'm going to. I've been hearing about this guy's temper, but right now he's acting like a big baby!"

"He won't for long." Leslie glanced at Battlecry. He'd flattened his ears menacingly at the reporter and taken a step forward. "Why don't you wait until I finish grooming him," Leslie suggested.

"Gotcha," the reporter said quickly. He'd seen the laid-back ears too. "I'll be down at the end of the barn." He beat a quick escape, looking nervously over his shoulder.

Leslie turned to Battlecry and started to laugh. "I think he was afraid you'd jump right out of the stall after him. You're such a show-off."

Battlecry huffed, then butted Leslie's idle hand with his nose.

"Yes, yes . . . I'll finish brushing you."

"Whew!" Leslie whispered to her father five hours later as they clutched lead shanks attached

169

to either side of Battlecry's bridle. He was trying his best to rear up between them as they moved him around the walking ring. "Come on . . . easy," she said to the horse. "I thought you were going to behave better today."

"He give you his promise on that?" her father asked sourly.

Leslie smiled. "Not exactly."

"At least this is normal. I just hope he gets most of it out of his system before he gets to the gate. We don't want a repeat of the last two races."

"Mmmm," Leslie agreed. She saw dozens of eyes and cameras focused on them and heard comments from the crowd. "He'll be burned up before he gets on the track," someone said.

"You've never seen him race before," someone else answered. "He's always like this."

"Just the same, I think I'll put my money on Zinger."

Leslie looked across the ring to Zinger. The big chestnut horse was following his groom like a perfect angel. Wishful seemed calm and collected as well. Only one other horse was showing a hint of Battlecry's temper, and he was a rank outsider. Battlecry suddenly threw up his head and gave a shrill whinny.

"Shhh," Leslie scolded.

"It's time to saddle him up," her father said. With his free hand, he motioned to Jeremy, who approached with the tack. The young groom didn't look too happy. He knew he'd have to help

Leslie hold the stallion while Mr. D'Andrea got the saddle in place. Battlecry wasn't about to make the saddling process easy. Leslie had to steady him with a firm hand on his shoulder as her father put on the pad, racing cloth, and saddle, and quickly tightened the girth while an official watched. Then Leslie and a very unhappy Jeremy led Battlecry off again. The jockeys had arrived, and Mr. D'Andrea walked over to talk to Karen. She listened intently. Karen knew what she could expect from the fractious stallion and was taking the ride seriously.

Then it was time for the jockeys to mount. Karen and Mr. D'Andrea walked over as Leslie and Jeremy struggled to steady Battlecry.

"He's full of it," Leslie said softly to Karen. "You'll really have to make sure you let him know who's boss."

Karen nodded and gave Leslie a quick smile. "I'm used to that by now. He's going to behave, and we're going to win it. Aren't we, big boy?"

Battlecry grunted and tried to fling up his head. Leslie jiggled on the lead, distracting him as Mr. D'Andrea gave Karen a leg into the saddle. The jockey quickly took up the reins and settled herself.

Leslie laid a gentle hand on Battlecry's muzzle and spoke softly in his ear. Amazingly, the stallion quieted for an instant. "Try to be a good boy today, all right? I believe in you, and I know you can win this race. I love you, monster." She kissed his nose, and Battlecry forgot himself long enough to nudge her shoulder affectionately.

"Did you see that!" someone cried from the crowd.

Leslie and Mr. D'Andrea led horse and rider toward the waiting escort ponies. "Good luck," Leslie called up to Karen.

"Thanks." She smiled. "See you in the winner's circle."

"Let's hope," Mr. D'Andrea said as he handed the lead shank to the escort rider. Battlecry was already dancing his muscular hindquarters in a sideways arc. The crowd quickly backed away from the fence, though there was no danger of Battlecry getting close enough to kick.

Mrs. D'Andrea hurried over, and the three of them started toward the grandstand and their reserved seats above the finish line. "Is it my imagination," she asked, "or is he worse than usual?"

"He's at least as bad as usual," her husband answered. "Maybe that's a good thing."

"At this point I don't even care if he wins," Mrs. D'Andrea said. "I just want to see him and Karen get through the race in one piece."

"Don't we all."

They pushed through the crowd toward their seats. The track was mobbed for the running of the Breeder's Cup races. There was a festive excitement in the air, and the seventh and most prestigious race was still to be run.

The field was parading by the stand by the time

the D'Andreas reached their seats. Leslie chewed her lip as she studied Battlecry's competition. Zinger was in the number two position. Wishful was five. The three-year-old who'd won that year's Kentucky Derby was running, as well as two older horses who had raced in the American Championship series, but Leslie didn't think they'd present much of a challenge. There were several European invaders, though, including D'Esprit and Sadler's Barron—winners of the top races in England and France. Battlecry had drawn the seventh post position in the twelve-horse field. Mr. D'Andrea would have been happier with a more inside position, but if Battlecry made a clean break, he should be able to pull clear of the rest of the field before the first turn.

The bettors obviously thought a lot of the European entries. They were second and third choices, tied with Zinger. Battlecry was going in as the 9 to 5 favorite. And he seemed to know it. Swaggering through the post parade, head and tail high, he electrified the crowd, but Leslie saw that his gleaming black coat was already marred by sweat patches. "Come on, boy, calm down a little," she whispered.

"It could be worse," her father said. "Though I won't breathe easy until he's out of the gate."

The field began their warm-up jog, circling the oval. The D'Andreas all raised their binoculars. Battlecry was moving smoothly, though Leslie groaned to see him snake out his head and try to nip the escort pony. Karen quickly tightened her right rein and pulled his head straight. All seemed to go well from there to the gate. The first three horses loaded. The escort rider had turned Battlecry over to two gate attendants, who would lead him in. Then suddenly Battlecry was up on his hind legs, pawing the air with his hooves. The gate attendants struggled with their shanks, trying to bring the big horse down. But this time Karen lost her seat. She tumbled over Battlecry's hindquarters onto the dirt of the track.

Leslie covered her mouth with her hand, stifling her cry. But Karen was instantly on her feet and brushed the dirt from her silks.

"Thank goodness," Mrs. D'Andrea gasped. "I guess she let down her guard. They've got him under control now. Karen's going to remount."

Leslie glanced to her father. He was frowning and his mouth was tight with tension.

"No more crazy stuff, Battle," Leslie pleaded as she watched Karen settle again in the saddle.

"Battlecry, fondly called the Terror of the Backside, is living up to his reputation," the announcer happily informed the crowd, "but he's going in calmly now."

Leslie wasn't so sure about the calm part. It took four attendants to get him in—two at his head, two with joined hands giving him a push from behind. But he and Karen were in. The doors were closed behind them. An attendant jumped up on the partition and grabbed Battle's ear. Quickly the remaining five horses loaded, but Leslie's eyes were glued to Battle. He was still fidgeting, and looked like a bomb ready to explode. She held her breath, waiting for the start of the race. Suddenly the bells sounded, and twelve gate doors flipped open. The race was on! But Battlecry had his head down. All eleven horses were out of the gate ahead of him—it was a repeat of his last race. Leslie heard her father curse softly.

14

"Battlecry is off a beat slow!" the announcer shouted. "As expected, Mystique has taken the lead, D'Esprit in second, Zinger placed nicely behind them in third, then Sadler's Barron, Justify. Then ten lengths back to . . ."

Leslie wasn't listening. Her only interest was Battlecry, who was quickly making up his lost ground, but was now faced with a wall of horses in front of him. Karen would either have to find a small opening or move him seven wide around the horses in front. It might not have been a problem if Battlecry was a horse who could be rated, and held off a fast pace. But he wasn't. He wanted to run near the front, or he didn't run at all, and the stallion would be boiling with frustration at being blocked.

"Take him around," Mr. D'Andrea muttered. "You haven't got any choice."

Karen obviously had the same thought in mind, and started swinging Battlecry wide. They were out in the middle of the track as the field came around the clubhouse turn. The extra distance they'd have to cover could take its toll later in the race, but Battlecry was happy now that he was passing horses. They started down the backstretch. The leaders had close to a fifteen-length advantage. Leslie's heart raced as she watched Battlecry's long strides start eating up the distance. Mystique still had the lead, but D'Esprit was gaining on his outside. Zinger had moved off the rail, ready to make his stand. Two lengths behind him, Sadler's Barron and Justify were running neck and neck. Battlecry was rapidly gaining on them, coming up on their outside.

The announcer's voice boomed in Leslie's ears. "They're coming into the far turn. D'Esprit has taken the lead, and Zinger's in gear now and is a close second off his flank! Mystique has dropped back to third. Sadler's Barron and Justify waiting to make their moves in fourth and fifth. And here comes Battlecry, *roaring* up on the outside. After a terrible start, the Terror is making up incredible ground! Farther back Wishful has found his best stride and is moving up quickly along the rail . . . and as they come into the far turn, it's Zinger now in the lead, but D'Esprit isn't giving up. He's battling back. They're neck and neck! Mystique hanging on to third with Sadler's Barron and Justify on his heels. They'll both need running room, and

177

Battlecry is moving up quickly outside of them!" The announcer's breath caught. "Wait! Justify has veered out badly! He's bumped Battlecry! The big black horse has stumbled!"

Leslie's heart slammed to her feet. She felt sick as she watched Karen swiftly steady Battlecry, but there was no chance now they could win.

"Karen Jenkins has masterfully steadied Battlecry," the announcer shouted, "but he's lost momentum and has dropped back to sixth. It looks like his chances of winning today are finished!"

"And as the field rounds the far turn, Zinger and D'Esprit are still fighting on the lead. Justify is a half length back in third, three more back to Wishful, Sadler's Barron, Mystique . . . and I don't believe it, folks! Battlecry is coming back! The big black horse isn't ready to quit. An unbelievable display of courage! And *down* the stretch they come!"

Leslie was screaming, although with the deafening roar in the stands, she couldn't hear her own voice. Battle was gaining with every stride. She could hardly believe what she was seeing. Not in a million years had she expected him to try to come back. "Come on, boy!" she screeched. "I love you!"

"They're at the sixteenth pole!" cried the announcer. "Zinger a nose in front of D'Esprit. And Battlecry is coming on like a freight train. A race for the history books! A true display of heart! And he's caught them! Yards from the wire, and the big black terror takes the lead. And he's under the wire! And he's won it! It's Battlecry by a length! Zinger, D'Esprit, Wishful. Never have I seen a performance like this! An absolutely amazing feat, an amazing career—from a horse who burst out of oblivion, who was almost destroyed for lack of talent! Today is definitely Battlecry's day!"

Tears of happiness were streaming down Leslie's cheeks as she fiercely hugged her parents. "He did it . . . he did it . . . he's wonderful . . . incredible!"

"He sure is!" Her mother's cheeks were streaked too. "I wouldn't have believed it if I hadn't seen it with my own eyes."

Leslie looked at her father's face. His eyes were wide and his mouth was hanging slightly open. He snapped it shut and swallowed. "I can't believe how he came back. To stumble like that and go on to win . . . that's heart . . . one hundred percent heart!"

Suddenly there was a startled cry from the crowd. "He's down!" the announcer gasped. "Battlecry's down!"

Leslie and her parents spun around to stare up the track. "No!" Leslie screamed. "No! It can't be!"

But it was. Battlecry had collapsed. He was lying motionless on the track. Karen was frantically bending over him. The other riders had stopped their mounts and stared in horror. An ambulance was already in motion.

15

Leslie and her parents clawed their way through the crowd, down the grandstand steps, and out to the track. They raced across the hoof-marked dirt with bursting lungs to the still immobile form of Battlecry.

Karen saw them coming. She rose from Battle's side to run toward them and throw herself sobbing in Mr. D'Andrea's arms. Horror marked the expressions of the others gathered near the fallen stallion. Someone was hurriedly setting up a folding cloth screen to shield the horse from the view of the distraught crowd in the grandstand.

Leslie flew across the remaining distance to fall on her knees beside the stallion's head. Even as she did, her worst fears seemed unspeakably confirmed. Battlecry hadn't moved—not a flicker of a muscle. He lay on his side, his slender legs partially extended. Leslie flung her arms around his

180

neck and pressed her face to his silky, sweat-dampened coat. "Battle! Oh, Battle!" she sobbed. Gently she lifted his sculpted head to cradle it on her lap. "I love you. Please be all right . . . please!"

The track vet quickly knelt at the fallen horse's side. His stethoscope was in place. He moved his hand to a pulse point, waited, listened. Battlecry's eyes were closed. He seemed peacefully asleep. Only a small and frightened corner of Leslie's mind acknowledged that Battlecry's sleek sides weren't lifting and falling as he drew breaths through his delicate nostrils. Instead, he was as still as sculpted stone. But it couldn't be! She felt the warmth of his body—the blood *had* to be coursing through his veins. In her mind, she saw him as he'd been moments before, courageously charging for the wire, his fine head stretched forward, his powerful muscles bunching, his legs pounding beneath him. So alive! So magnificent! No, this stillness wasn't real! He had to be alive. Repeatedly she stroked his head, his neck, praying.

The vet leaned away from Battlecry's side and looked over to her. His expression was drawn. He let out a ragged sigh and shook his head sadly. Leslie saw the glint of wetness in his eyes. "He's gone," he said hoarsely. "A massive coronary, I'd say."

"No!" Leslie screamed. "No! He can't be dead!

No, Battle, no! You can't die! I love you! I can't lose you!"

The vet reached over and laid his hand on hers. "I'm sorry. I know how you feel."

"No, you don't!"

"The death of a young horse is always tragic . . . especially so with a horse of this caliber, under these circumstances. If it's any comfort at all, it was fast. He wouldn't have suffered. His last feeling was probably the exultation of winning."

Leslie could only stare at the vet as her shoulders shook with racking sobs. He was lying. This kindly man was lying. Battlecry couldn't be dead. Dimly she was aware of others kneeling beside her. She heard other heartbroken cries. Someone placed a hand on Leslie's shoulder, but she shook it away and dropped her face again to Battlecry's neck, tangling her fingers in his long mane. "Please don't be dead . . . *please* . . . oh, Battlecry!" It was a scream of utter grief, but Leslie didn't know she was screaming.

"Leslie," a choked, tear-laden voice called in her ear. "Sweetheart." It was her mother's voice. "You . . . you can't do anything for him now."

"No, I'm not leaving him! No!"

Leslie's father knelt at her side and put an arm around her shoulders. "Go ahead, cry . . . cry it out—" His voice cracked. It was several seconds before he could speak again. "I can't believe it either. He gave everything he had for us . . . for you, really. He loved you, or he wouldn't have tried so hard."

"And he died because of it!" Leslie wailed.

"No. Don't think that! He wanted to race. He wanted to win. It's what made him happy. He died knowing he was the best."

"He is the best . . . he is . . ." But Leslie could no longer deny the truth. Her beloved stallion wasn't going to get up. He was dead, and there was an empty, aching hole inside her that couldn't be filled. Battlecry wasn't just a horse. He was a personality—as human as any of the people gathered around him now.

"They have to take him off the track," her father said gently. "You'll have to leave him now."

"Please . . . let me say good-bye," she whispered. "Please . . . just me and Battle."

She didn't look up, but she knew the adults around her had risen and moved away. She gently stroked Battlecry's head, lovingly memorizing each plane and hollow. She slid her fingers through the thatch of black mane between his ears and smoothed it. "You'll never be dead to me, Battle. You'll always be alive inside me. You showed the whole world what love and courage are all about, and they'll never forget it . . . or you. Oh, God, I'm going to miss you so much!" she gasped. "It hurts so bad!" Tears blurred her vision. She leaned down and kissed his forehead, smelling his scent, feeling the silkiness of his hair against her cheek. Then with a gasping sob, she rose, took one last look at her beloved horse, and fled from behind the screen. Her parents were waiting, and they wrapped their arms around her.

Leslie walked slowly across the icy pasture behind the barn. The sky overhead was leaden gray, and the air hitting her cheeks was so cold it stung. Over a month had passed since the tragic race—in fact, it was Christmas Eve, though Leslie didn't feel any of the season's cheer. Her grief hadn't gone away. Repeatedly she woke from nightmares of that horrible moment when she'd looked up the track to see Battle down . . . Karen kneeling over him. The racing world had been grief-stricken too. Headlines had blared out the loss: "RACE OF THE DECADE ENDS IN TRAGEDY," "THE RACING WORLD MOURNS A HERO." Her parents and the farm staff had been grief-stricken and stunned. Her friends had cried. But no one felt the loss like she did.

She reached the end of the pasture, protected by a towering and ancient oak tree. Beneath the tree was Battlecry's grave. Marking the grave was a polished block of marble, crowned by a metal sculpture of Battlecry, tail raised, mane flying. She read the inscription beneath, as she had done so many times before. "His courage and heart should be a lesson to us all. You are not forgotten, Battlecry."

All of a sudden Leslie's eyes welled with tears. She couldn't keep crying forever, but there were times, like this, when she just couldn't stop. She tried to remind herself that Battlecry's death had brought good, too. Two more rescue farms had been set up in Battle's honor, and so many contributions had come in that the D'Andreas would never have to worry about funding their farm again. But she missed him! She missed his wild antics. She missed flying like the wind on his back. She missed his infrequent gentle moments when he let her kiss his nose or hug his neck. The stables seemed so still and lifeless with Battle gone.

Footsteps came up behind her, crunching on the icy layer of snow. Her father walked up and put his hand on her shoulder. "I think you should come to the barn," he said. "I've got a surprise for you."

"I don't want another horse." Since Battle's death both her parents had been trying to direct her interest to another rescue horse.

"You might want this one. Come on."

Leslie followed mechanically as they walked back to the barn. It seemed she'd done everything automatically for the last month and a half. Inside the barn, her father led her along the hay- and horse-scented aisle to a big box stall. Her mother, Jeremy, and Edwin were standing outside. They were all smiling. Edwin motioned with his head. "Take a look in there."

Leslie walked to the stall door and looked over. The black mare, Exotic Halo, stood at the rear. At her feet was curled a still damp black bundle, all head and legs. The newborn foal's head was up and its ears were pricked as it stared at Leslie.

"A little boy," Edwin said. "Image of his daddy, like I thought. A few weeks early, but I can't see anything wrong with him. Feisty little fella, in fact. He's already been up to eat. He's just resting now."

The foal flicked his fuzzy, oversize ears. Leslie couldn't stop herself—she went inside. With a melting heart, she knelt down on the straw beside the foal. Her eyes filled with tears again, but this time, of both sadness and joy. Reaching out a hand, she stroked the foal's tiny, ink-black side. He turned his head and nuzzled her hand. "You do look just like him," she said with a sigh.

The foal trustingly laid his head on her leg. Leslie scratched his ears and ran her finger down the length of his tiny head. "Oh, if only you were here to see this, Battle," she whispered. "But maybe you aren't gone after all. Your spirit's right here, living on, isn't it?"

As if in answer, Battlecry's son nudged her fingers and blew softly through his delicate nostrils. Leslie leaned down and gently hugged him. For the first time in weeks, some of the emptiness inside was filled. The foal was beautiful—absolutely beautiful. He was just like a miniature Battlecry.

"I know what I'm going to call you," she murmured to the tiny animal, "so your father knows he's not forgotten. You're Son of Battle—and I know you're going to live up to the name."

The tiny horse lifted his head and butted it firmly into Leslie's stomach.

"Yes, you're going to live up to it all right." She smiled.